Prince of India
The Beginning

By
Abhi Kandukuru

Copyright © 2012 by Abhishek Kandukuru

Printed in the United States of America

First Printing: 7th, November 2012

Freedom Press
ISBN-13: 978-0988628397
ISBN-10: 0988628392
ISBN-13: 978-1480297227
ISBN-10: 1480297224
Library of Congress Control Number: 2012954316
BISAC: Fiction / Action & Adventure

Tanri hepinizi korusun
May God bless all

To my family and the people I know

Surya's Life

Born as a Prince, Surya was created by God, born inside his mother. With the swift speed of a horse, the strength of god and the mind of Brahma, the creator, these powers given to him by the Indian God of Destruction help him as he fights against the evil in the world. The Indian God of Destruction became his guardian god for his lifetime.

But before all that, as a child he was accepted in Abgabeschule, the Royalty School in Berlin, Germany. While he was away from home, his country would fall under the control of tyrants. So he created a robot that looked and acted like a human. Unfortunately at Abgabeschule, his amazing ability to create such machines gave him the reputation of being a geek and he was constantly being bullied. That's how he met Amber Shellington, the woman who would become his girlfriend.

After he returned to his homeland, his robot creation fought with him. The robot was created to protect the country from evil. But as it grew arrogant, it was finally killed by Surya's guards but not before shooting Surya in the chest while he was trying to save his father.

Later, Surya brings Pooja, his sister, Tommy, his best friend, the Prince of Monaco, and Amber, his girlfriend and the President of the United States daughter, to help save Istanbul, the city on the Golden Horn, from the robot's army, the Notrax. His friends fight with Surya as he wages war with the robots. This is his story, and theirs.

Laroche's Life

Captain Alexander Laroche is the antagonist of the Prince of India Trilogy. Created by the hands of Surya, he was built and programmed to defend the country of India as one of the Notrax. He was originally known as Dushyant, meaning the Destroyer of Evil. He was built like a human, an American, and has human attributes. After he was built, Surya inserted data inside Laroche's artificial brain—data that makes him do things that humans can do, and things that humans cannot do. Although Laroche was a robot, Surya treated him like he was part of the family.

As Surya grew, Laroche grew up with him but became arrogant as he grew hungry for power. He wants to rule India all for himself. His attempt to kill the King of India injures Surya, but also causes him to end up on the scrap heap, discarded and disgraced.

After one year, he was found by an Iranian General named Kazem Zahaar as he was looking for powerful weapons to make him invincible. General Zahaar fixed him and immediately set up a partnership with Laroche. Laroche built an entire devastating army and became known as the "Destroyer of the Good" as a worldwide terrorist.

Prologue

Laroche murdered him. Infuriated that her father wouldn't answer how I got here, he simply killed him. And shot me. After I had been shot and thrown off a dragon, I came to my senses to find myself out in a forest. It was a painful experience. The bullet had caused a massive injury, and subsequently caused an infection. The smell arising from the wound was rotten, and the sight of it was revolting. The bullet obviously came from a biotech weapon. The pain was unbearable, and watching my blood leak from my shoulder made me realize that trying to move had been a bad idea. I couldn't walk at all. The poison from the bullet seeping into my body made my legs numb. The pain was colossal in comparison to the injury I had suffered back at the city.

I found a thick branch on the ground and got the matches from my pocket. I still remember how I got them. But that's a story for another time. As the chemicals started to course through my body, my vision failed and I couldn't see a thing. I began to hallucinate, seeing visions of people dear to me who had died and passed on. I could see the Sultan right next to me. He encouraged me not to give up.

I was halfway through the forest and the constant drum of the rain and the thundering was rending my ears. I fell to the ground, cupping my hands to the sides of my head. I experienced pain in my body and once again I couldn't walk, so I was forced to crawl to find my way to a nearby shelter. I had the sense that a cave was nearby. A gut feeling. I forced my eyes to open, but saw nothing but bright pinpoints of light. When my eyes finally started to focus, everything became clear. I discovered I had been right after all. A cave was there, to rest for the night.

As I rested, I attempted to touch my injury. Every time I felt it, it stung more than if a monster-sized bee had spiked its stinger into me. I thought it was worth it, saving the one I love from any danger. "It's okay, Surya. You did it for love," I thought.

My vision started to worsen again by the moment. I was losing focus and seeing objects as blurry pixels again. There was something there, in the cave with me. What was it? I saw a silhouette and a weird-looking object next to it. My eyes closed as I fell to the ground.

Chapter I
The Beginning

"Never interrupt your enemy when he is making a mistake."
    -Napoleon Bonaparte

Wars are not started by people of good intent, but by people who make the worst mistakes of their life. In this case, I am the reason why a war will start in the future. I am twenty-one years old, yet I still don't know what to expect from anything.

Oh, wait, I haven't told you who I am yet. My name is Surya, and I am the Prince of India. I defend most of the world from anything that threatens innocent people. But for the last two years I have been fighting to defend any country as it falls under the control of the Notrax, a terrorist organization. They are robots that walk like humans, that appear as humans do, but they are not humans. They have been turning our world into a hellhole. This is the war I have started. By creating one robot that has changed the world in a negative way.

Obviously, this was not my intent.

It was nine years ago when I was only twelve. I studied Robotics my first year at Abgabeschule, a German school meant for the Royalty of the world. I built a robot that could fight for freedom with me. I injected my DNA into his system so he could have the same powers as me. The same strength, the same mental power, the same speed. He was like a clone, in many ways. Except for his metal insides. And the fact that I made him appear American. I had my reasons for that. I named him Dushyant.

However, as I trained him, I treated him like the brother I never had. He became a member of our family. He would help my sister whenever I was busy. He would help my mother and father with their work. He continuously cheered me up whenever things were bad. Most of all he was always there for me, and for that I loved him as I loved my family.

Maybe that is why I couldn't see the changes.

After a span of two years, he became hungry for power of his own as my family and he ruled the

Kingdom of Vidarbha together. He began to grow selfish and wanted everything to come to him instantly, to have what he wanted handed to him. I kept quiet because I was so attached to him that I couldn't think badly of him. Sadly, it came to a point where I could no longer ignore it. There came the day when he would have to be terminated.

He visited a local gun shop with the intent to purchase a weapon to assassinate somebody. Who that someone was remained a mystery to me at the time. Of course, that was not the reason he told me for his trip. He had told me he'd be back with the weapons and armor needed to advance upon the guards to protect the village and the marketplace. So, he went, grabbed assault rifles and body armor, and armed himself.

Dushyant returned with a gun in his hand. It had a laser pointer, which he aimed at my father's forehead.

As he pulled the trigger, the bullet sped towards the King's forehead. And I, without thinking, jumped into the path of that bullet as quickly as possible. I was not fast enough. My father had been shot in his lower abdomen. And I was shot in my chest.

Dushyant smiled, proud of himself. His moment of admiring himself did not last long before he was shot twenty times in the heart by two heavy armored guards wielding machine guns. I was taken to the hospital immediately and Dushyant was taken to the dumpster in which all trash must go. The bullet had exited through my flesh cleanly and the doctor said no worries. The pain was minimized in my body because of the amazing abilities I had been born with, but the anger was just beginning to boil up inside of me, and for that there was no cure. I had a bad feeling in my stomach that throwing away the robot might have been a bad idea.

Two months later, I saw Dushyant's picture splashed on the covers of various newspapers, sporting headlines such as "The Corruptor of Countries" and "Called by His New Name, Captain Laroche." Given the abilities of my mind for creating, he had created an army of robots that looked like humans, but with the power to destroy entire cities.

This is the beginning of the story. But only the beginning.

Chapter II
The Attack

"An invasion of armies can be resisted, but not an idea whose time has come."
-Victor Hugo

Wires were being cut and plugged inside the humanoid. To watch him, one would have thought this was a normal routine, but this time it was anything but. He had been planning to lead his brother into a trap that would kill him. General Kazem Zahaar, the Iranian general, was just fixing Laroche with a few final adjustments in his metal body.

"All tidy and neat," General Zahaar said. "This should do it. Your inertial sensors are alright, the Li-Polymer battery is fine, and main computers one and two are working fine. You'll be ready for the Invasion."

Laroche was pleased to hear that. "Good. Gather up all weapons and artillery. Submarine guns, machine guns, every explosive or weapon you see in the headquarters. Then I can call it ready."

"All Notrax aircraft troops, report to launching area. All ground troops, report to docks with the Notrax marine groups. We must leave at midnight, I repeat we must leave at midnight." announces Laroche as all the Notrax troops gathered tanks, missiles, and mechanical creatures of all sorts. Each robot is programmed with data that no other human has. Battle plans, maps, information, and so on.

The Notrax are a knavish army, built to terrorize the world after Surya crushed Laroche's feelings by throwing him away. Terrorizing almost half the world, the Notrax were used to invading and conquering countries.

The army soon was reaching Istanbul, the port city and the capital of Turkey in the Middle East. As they were flying in a cargo plane, four soldiers known by the name of Bladeface, Viper, Screamer, and Dark Archer had been preparing themselves for the invasion. These four were trained and had been ready for this moment since the beginning of their lives.

Bladeface, the master assassin, wielded all different kinds of blades. He had an aimbot installed into his eyes so that he would never miss a shot.

Screamer is a normal Notrax soldier but she screeches into a victim's ear so loud, that the person's face would blow up.

Dark Archer is an archer who wields different kinds of bows and crossbows. Like her brother Bladeface, she also had an aimbot installed in her eyes, ensuring she never misses a shot.

And Viper is the robot that bears robotic snakes, which can kill a person in less than a minute. Its venom is filled with neurotoxins, an extremely deadly poison. These four assassins are very hard to kill.

By the time Laroche had reached there, the sky had become as black as oil. Darkness filled the air over Turkey when they reached the palace. It was too silent. Way too silent. Laroche was planning an ambush to attack the back portion of the palace. "Viper, go up first. Scale the wall. I will attack with the rest of the army. I want to see a few guards dead or else..." Laroche firmly spoke.

Viper charged up the wall as Dark Archer, Viper's sister, shot gold-tipped arrows at the wall for him to use as handholds. The remaining four went up the wall. When they reached the platforms, Dark Archer got her field crossbow ready, Viper got his mechanical cobras, pythons, and other snakes ready, Bladeface got his swords, daggers, and blades and Screamer raised her voice to deathly high volume.

The first guard approached and Viper shot his cobra at the guard's face, poisoning him. Another guard was alerted by the guard's screams as the cobra gnawed the face. Dark Archer shot her first arrow at the guard. "No, Screamer, don't do it!" Dark Archer exclaimed, knowing what she was about to do.

Screamer grabbed the guard and screamed in his ear as his face blew up. After she screamed, all the guards were alerted and the assassins, including Laroche, got their weapons ready. "Look what you did, you idiot!" Laroche yelled at her.

As the guards spread out, Bladeface shot five blades at each guard and threw a dagger at one of the guard's chest, then fought on with two dwarven battle swords.

"Viper, take that section," Laroche ordered. "Signal the army when I have opened gate one. Pull up your map so you know which one to open. Then signal me so I can call the rest of the army in."

Both brothers went their separate ways. Bladeface grabbed the oil well's rope and leaped. The oil spilled and poured onto the entire Turkish army. Bladeface threw a torch in the oil while it was still pouring and created a fiery weapon. The people were screaming with terror and fiery breaths. The guards' flesh burned away down to their skeletons. The blood burned and spilled red.

Viper signaled the army and they raged through the desert and into the marketplace, riding on their robot horses, murdering people and killing the guards.

The Princess of Turkey came rushing out of her rooms in the Palace after hearing the treacherous sounds of the people dying. She heard someone coming upstairs so she wrote a quick letter and gave it to the messenger, "Take this message to the Prince of India and make sure he gets it."

Laroche, Zahaar and the four assassins were right in front of the Sultan. Bladeface took his blade and placed it near the Sultan's neck.

"Now, now, Bladeface! Calm down," General Zahaar said with a smile. "We don't want our beloved Sultan and his lovely daughter to die, now do we?"

Bladeface put his blade down, and snarled at the Sultan.

Laroche stepped up close to the Sultan. "Look, I'll make this as simple as possible. Do you know why I am invading this country?"

There was an awkward moment of silence. While the Sultan was thinking, two Turkish guards began to run, but Laroche shot them with the built in pistols inside his body. Princess Kyla looked at the guards, her face sickened.

"A hole in the head. That never gets old," Laroche said. "Now, your attractive daughter of yours is telling me the answer to the question I asked you." The Sultan had no answer, yet Laroche saw the fear in his eyes. "Reason why is that this country will soon fall under my control, and you will be Sultan no more. I will finally get to wear that silly hat of yours.

Laroche headed to the window and saw the terror in the marketplace. "Ah, do you just smell the happiness in the air? That happiness will continue as long as I am in control."

"Oh, then you must be blind or you don't have a sense of smell!" yelled Princess Kyla.

Laroche winked at Kyla's disgust. "I like this girl's attitude. Anyway, in the next two months, I will take over the throne, and marry your daughter. Meanwhile, order the citizens to fall under the control of the great robot general, so that I may spare your life. I asked you to give me your throne, and your life is spared. Nevertheless, threats like the US Navy Seals or the Black Operations Team or worse can harm us, leaving us no choice but to show you the consequences. Therefore, if I tell you this once, I am telling you this a thousand times. You call anyone for assistance, and you will not be waking up ever again. Understood?"

The Sultan nodded as he shook in fear.

"Great. You know what I expect. This will be my country, and my palace. A change will rise in this country and, you know what that is? A new Sultan."

The six soldiers left the palace and rode off with the remainder of the army. The Sultan trembled in fear as he went to his departed father's photo for help. He felt so sad. He was crouching with his head down. Tears dripped down his cheek and he fell to the ground, kneeling in front of the mural. "Oh dear father, I do not know what happened. My country is dead. The soldiers are dead. What should I do? I ask your help and the gods that are with you."

The Princess of Turkey looked out her window. She saw people sobbing. People dead. "Dad, we have backup. Do not cry. The Prince of India is coming to fight just for us."

The sultan immediately stood up and said, "What? Kyla, You have made a grave mistake. You heard what the robot said, if there is any threat here to destroy them, he will kill me. I am scared. What will happen?"

Kyla calmed him down. "Nothing will happen. I know that because they call him the mighty warrior of the world who will not accept death until he has finished a nation's request for help."

At six o'clock before midday, the Sultan's messengers posted a letter on every telephone pole and house as a message to the Prince of India:

Citizens of Istanbul, you shall not be fearful of the tyrant. We will have revenge, and your relatives shall be avenged as well. Help will come. Help will come.

Chapter III
The Message

"My message to you all is of hope, courage and confidence. Let us mobilize all our resources in a systematic and organized way and tackle the grave issues that confront us with grim determination and discipline worthy of a great nation."
    -Muhammad Ali Jinnah

Twenty-one years later, the Kingdom of Vidarbha was nearly unrecognizable after years of war. Matters are horrible in the kingdom. Food was running out and somehow the local water supply had been infected with a virus. All we can hope on are the other countries that will trade food with us and we can find a better water source.

It was five o'clock in the morning. It was still dark out. All the roadside shops were closed and some people slept next to it. You could hear the leaks in the shacks dripping on the ground and the stray dogs howling in the distance. I quickly slipped into my clothes and went down to the kitchen to make myself soup for the morning as the chefs were asleep at their own houses.

I exited the palace doors and walked through the marketplace as if I was taking a Sunday stroll. As I was walking, I felt a threat behind me. I could sense it in the silence behind me. This was a different kind of silence, and I felt a cool breeze charging towards my body. Something was behind me.

Suddenly I heard panting and felt pointy ears. I turned to my left and found a pairs of eyes, yellow and fierce looking, hiding in the dark. I aim my bow and arrow and shoot it in its eye. The thing whimpers while I take out another arrow and set it. I had a feeling it was a golden wolf as they roam in packs now around the kingdom after they were genetically engineered to hunt down any vermin that might harm the city. The lab thought they were protectors, but they ended up as predators of the kingdom.

I go into the meadows of the kingdom to hunt as most of the woodland creatures are there. The meadows are a peaceful place in the kingdom. No humans are allowed to go here, naturally, due to the barrier that protects the meadows from the forbidden wastelands of India. Flowers grow there and deer roam around in herds to eat the healthy grass on the ground. Forests spread around different parts of the meadows. The cool breeze comes everyday at this time and goes away five seconds later.

As I climbed the trees to get a better view of the forest, I saw no animals roaming around. Usually during the summer, squirrels chase each other for nuts, deer eat the grass around the grassy meadow and coyotes roam around in packs. But today, I did not see any animals around. I ran on the tree's branches to see if I could find anything else around the forest. As soon as I got to the last tree in the forest, I found a rabbit, wandering around the end of the forest and leaping onto the remains of a tree that had been cut down.

I jumped off the branch and silently landed on the grass. I camouflaged with the tall grass and moved into the forest. I hid behind the tree, which the rabbit was on, and I grabbed it by its ears. It was struggling to escape and was squirming around. As I cupped its bottom for support, I heard the muffled sounds of kicking. I realized that there was another creature living inside of it.

I was surprised I would find one because of the emptiness of the meadow's forest, but I felt sorry for torturing this poor animal. It felt like it was a sin to kill females and younglings.

"You have another creature about to come out in the real world, don't you? Why should I torture you when you have gone through so much? Here, I'll let you go, so you'll have a happy life." I spoke to the rabbit as I pushed it lightly. There was a rule in our kingdom: never hurt females or younglings. In addition, for those who do not follow, there are consequences, such as banishment, execution, or a five-year sentence in jail. Those who followed got nothing but respect from the kingdom.

After accidentally torturing that poor rabbit, I lost my interest for hunting but I couldn't go back without some game. So, I decided to stalk one more animal and to kill it so I could give it to the butcher and he would trade it with other countries. As I was up in the trees, I found my target. It was a deer, a male one fully-grown, strong and with full sized antlers. I got my bow ready with my arrow and had my mind focused on the target. I aimed the arrow to its body. I had the kill when all of a sudden, a person came yelling my name, "Surya! Surya!"

The kill was gone, and the deer escaped as fast as it could. "Damn it! What is it?"

"It's Princess Kyla. She wants you to read this letter as request for help."

Princess Kyla? What does she want?" I felt like this must be an urgent letter.

"Let me see that."

Dear Surya,

I need your help. Laroche invaded Istanbul, and I thought it would be best if I called you. Please help. Please.

Signed,
Princess Kyla

"Tell Pooja to pack her suitcase. I'll pack mine up once we get to Istanbul."

I rushed to the palace as fast as possible to pack up my stuff, as Nitin, the second trainer of the soldiers and also my close friend, booked the tickets for the Galata Express so that I could take a boat across the strait. As I went back, Pooja was at the door, waiting for me. "Surya, why are going?"

"We have to go now. We have to pick up Amber and Tommy right now and get on the Galata Express. I'll tell to you on the train," I told her as I packed up my clothes.

"We're ready," Pooja told me.

Chapter IV
The Journey

"Do the difficult things while they are easy and do the great things while they are small. A journey of a thousand miles must begin with a single step."
    -Lao Tzu

It was a note I had to respond to. It was a call for help. I was surprised that he had the power to attack the entire city, as most of his inventions fail. But enough of that, I thought to myself. These innocent people were in trouble and I had to figure out a way to stop him from destroying the city. But, I knew it wasn't a one man job. I had to call two of my best friends, and as I like to call one of them, my brother.

There was Thomas Clairoux, alias Tommy, the Prince of Monaco and very young. His reputation for genius is due to his engineering skills and the technology he builds, such as the barriers that surround Monaco and defend the country. They also have built-in machine guns that shoot from any angle. He also made the automated HMGs that shoot without a person controlling it. All of these were built by Tommy to make Monaco the most heavily protected country in Europe. But that wasn't the real reason I wanted Tommy with me. Tommy and me were best friends since the day we were born, being born on the same day. After that coincidence, my mother and father became friends with the King and Queen of Monaco. But the only place we would hang out would be at school. He would always be there for me whenever there was a problem that needed to resolved.

Then there was my other best friend. Her name was Amber Shellington, and she was the President of the United States' daughter. At the age of fifteen, I dated her at Abgabeschule, the Royalty School. She was beautiful, and kind, and never bowed down to her enemies. In fact, she never consider betraying those she felt loyalty to. The last time I saw her, she had dirty blonde hair, and she wore a t-shirt and jeans everyday back at Abgabeschule. But we haven't seen each other in a very long time. And time changes a person.

"Why are you rushing over to Monaco?" Tommy questioned me as I pulled up the map of Istanbul.

"Look, it's because I need to save Istanbul. Kyla is my friend. That, and I feel responsible for creating that metal scrap. I need to fix the troubles I've caused, so that's why I need help from Amber and you, along with Pooja."

"You had to call Amber, Surya? You know that she hates me after stealing her Uzi just to upgrade my wall. I was willing to let it go. But no, she had to use her speed to maul me after chasing me around."

Dying from laughter, I remembered the time he spoke of, the craziest day of my life. "Yeah, you stole her favorite hot pink Uzi,"

"But only for a good reason!" he objected as I was recovering from the stitch in my side from laughing to death.

I was arriving at the station of the French Quail Express to pick up Tommy at Monaco Castle. After ten minutes, I was at the International Train Station to depart the Monaco Express. The station was packed with people during the rush hour. Ladies sat on the smooth concrete ground, making Jasmine hair ornaments, selling them for fifteen rupees each. Seems like they weren't doing so good. Others were selling foods fried in boiling hot oil such as Indian Dumplings and the crispy flatbread. People were leaning on the pillars that held the roof up and calling to each other. Others were running to catch their train, carrying huge suitcases filled with their essential needs.

"All aboard the Monaco Express!" the conductor yelled as I grabbed Pooja's hand and dashed to the next open door.

As we get inside the train, we sat down in our seats. "Surya, where are we going?" Pooja asked me.

I was going to have to tell her now. Taking a deep breath, I said the words before I lost my nerve. "Yesterday, there was an invasion that destroyed almost the entire country of Turkey. Princess Kyla, daughter of Sultan Byziwad, wrote this note to me as a request for help." I showed it to her, waited for her to read it. "I thought I should go, but with your powers, I decided to take you, too. But I also called Tommy and Amber to help me as I might need them."

Pooja didn't seem okay with that as she was sweating and her face looked nervous. In fact, I think she was scared after I told her in detail about the Invasion and how the robot I created was out trying to hunt me down and kill me.

Palais du Prince
Monaco

It was a matter of time before the next train to United States arrived to depart from the Monaco Station. As we got off the train, it was nothing like the station back at India. The floor was swept every five minutes to prevent dirt from collecting. Men were in suits, wearing Richard Mille watches, and wearing various colors of scarfs. The ladies were all fancy in their heels and their beautiful dresses. They had their hair straightened or curled up to attract rich men.

The Palais du Prince, or in English, The Palace of the Prince, is the building in which the Prince of Monaco lives. After every country in Africa, Asia, and Europe came into a monarchy due to rules the United Nations formed, they've became the second most protected country in the world. But after the rule was declared, Tommy's parents were assassinated by a Mexican Drug Dealer, leaving him alone. He now rules the country, and developed it a lot, bringing high tech weapons that are not controlled by humans, and robots built to protect the palace (although, I thought that was the worst idea) and people being doctored and healed by machines, all but replacing humans.

Once I went inside, I felt so different as I walked through the hall, as if I was walking through an entire training area. There was a long blue carpet that led to the throne where Tommy was sitting with his computer and his gadgets on his side.

"Knock, knock." I said to inform Tommy of my presence. Tommy looked up and his eyes started to widen as he smiled at me. He came up and hugged me. We hadn't seen each other for years. He had long hair like mine except his was brown and he was wearing an American Eagle T-Shirt with dark Jeans on. People called him "The Hunk of Monaco" but as we both agreed on, he wasn't one at all.

"Now this is not some kind of vacation, so I would suggest you bring your computer and your weapons. Got it?" I said to him.

But as usual, Tommy was prepared for the trip already. He had his rifle and revolver in a case, his computer inside his backpack and his clothes and other stuff in two suitcases. I handed him his two tickets to board on the District of Columbia

Express. So after we picked up Tommy from the Palais du Prince, we headed off to the Monaco Station to go over to Washington D.C, the birthplace of my long- time-no-see girlfriend.

Washington D.C
The United States
of America

"Arriving at the District of Columbia Train Station. Next train, Istanbul Express at 4:30 PM. All passengers must exit through the designated gate given. Please pick up bags near the gate."

The intercom at the train station broadcast the main announcements as Tommy, Pooja and I located our place on the map. The train station was full of many diverse people. Indians, French, Mexicans, Spanish, you name it. It looked like an airport, but also a little bit similar to the Subway in New York City. The place was kept neat and orderly. There were street performers with people gathered around them laughing as they made jokes. Hobos were on the side of chairs, drinking beer and liquor. They were wearing rags for clothes and had old blankets for sleeping. Although they smelled, I felt bad for them and decided to give them something. So I walked over to one of the beggars and I gave him my blanket, my pillow, and two hundred dollars, "Use it for food and water, my good man."

"May God bless you, child." he said while crying tears of joy.

"OK, so where are we going to find Amber?"

Pooja inquired as I was busy looking at the map.

"Surya!" Tommy exclaimed to grab my attention.

"Whoa, what the hell?" I yelled, caught in my deep trance. I knew where Amber was. She would be in the White House, but I had tried calling her and she wouldn't answer. My phone wouldn't even let me leave a voice message.

After ten minutes, we reached the White House. I saw many guards on the roof with sniper rifles and strong canines guarding the White House with their masters. As Tommy, Pooja and I walked through the gate of the White House, two guards with heavy armor were waiting at the front and pointed their gun at me. United States Secret Service agents trying to protect the President. To show them I was an ally for the President, I pulled out my Royal Council License and I told them that Tommy and Pooja were with me.

The guards led me through the White House to the Residence in the East Wing. I rang the doorbell and I heard her beautiful voice, the voice that lures me directly to her.

"Dad, I got the door!"

Then I saw her in front of me, looking different than before. Her eyes were still the same blue, but somehow looking more beautiful than before. Her skin shone brighter than the light of stars and I was caught in her beauty. Her hair was straight and brown. She definitely wasn't a teenager anymore. She was a woman.

"Dad, it's for you! I need to know your name before I can tell him that one of his friends is here, so may I?" she asked me in her sweet voice.

"My name is Surya," I told her.

I saw her stop, running the name through her mind, pulling up old memories. She looked me up and down carefully. "Surya, is it really you?" she asked, a questioning expression on her face.

I nodded and her eyes widened as she smiled. She hugged me tightly and I returned it, lifting her off the ground, feeling that love again in my heart. To be honest, as her hair was touching my face, her arms tight around me, it felt so good that I felt like confessing my true feelings to her.

"Where were you for the past five years?" she asked me. "God, I've missed you so freakin' much! So what brings you here?"

I told her everything then, even though it brought pain to my heart. I would rather protect her. Her and the rest of my team. Who knows what could happen?

I gave her the note instead of telling her the main reason why I was here. After she read the whole thing, her jaw dropped and she started shaking in fear. She cupped her hand to her mouth, feeling angry, reading the note over and over again, "Who would do something like this?"

"Um... Laroche. Pay attention, Amber!" Tommy responded, trying to prove her stupid.

Pulling a knife, she put it near his neck, and whispered in a deadly voice, "I will kill you, Tommy. And I want my Uzi back!"

I calmed Amber down. Tommy had sweated through his shirt. "You may want to change your shirt, Tommy," I said with a small smile.

"And probably my pants cause I just went to the bathroom." Tommy said, and I couldn't tell if he was serious or joking.

Amber pulled back the knife, giggling at her revenge on Tommy. After a few minutes she had her suitcase packed up. She told her butler that she would come back in a month and asked him to tell her parents that she was leaving on a business trip. The Butler seemed to be okay with that, and he left the room without saying anything.

So the journey started. All four of us left the White House and took one of the official cars to board the Trans-continent Express.

A few minutes later, we came to the station. We were stuck waiting for the next train. We waited for a while, until I went to go check as it was taking too long. Princess Kyla was waiting there, expecting my arrival.

As I was walking, I saw this old lady pop up in front of me. She looked like a hag, missing all of her teeth except three in the front. She was wearing rags as clothes and she was using a thick branch as her cane. I looked at her face and she had one eye. The other socket was hollow. Her voice was raspy hand squeaked as she tried to tell me something important. Her hand touched mine and she put something inside of it.

"Take this to reveal in your journey. You are hope for Istanbul."

What the…? How did she know I was...? It was truly indeed some sort of Sorcery, I thought.

After two hours waiting for the train, we finally hopped on as I thought, the war now commences.

Chapter V
The Crash

"You take a crash, you get back up and next time you succeed and that's a great feeling."
  -Shaun White

Back at their headquarters, Laroche's men were going through their maps and manning Robot Golems that scan for any person who looks like a threat to the Notrax. Unless Laroche powers down the Golems, not even Surya has a chance of surviving. Robot Golem Patrols are heavy armored robots that patrol a given region that has been assigned to them by Laroche. These robots are equipped with machine guns on one arm and built-in cannons in the other one. Like all of the other Notrax robots, these patrols have been programmed with an aimbot in their system. Golem Patrols are very hard to kill.

The map room of the Notrax Headquarters was filled with large monitors and maps. Each robot took over a position to man the Patrol

Golems and the cannons with their built-in cameras. As Surya and his friends were on the Turkish Express, Notrax troops scanned the train through video and they saw Surya and his friends on the train. As the Notrax's main objective was to eliminate him, a messenger ran as fast as he could to inform Laroche. "Captain, he has just entered Turkey through Edirne. Should we attack?"

Laroche was resting in his chamber where he did his meditating. At the messenger's word he rose off the yoga mat to say, "Alert the Golems. Make sure there are no survivors in the train. Those Golems must use cannons. Alert them, now!"

"As you wish, Captain."

The messenger went to the control room and alerted the Golems as Laroche had commanded. "You have a train, coming your way. Captain Laroche needs you to eliminate it. Make sure there are no survivors!"

The Golems snarl to the troops as it starts to attack. The Turkish Express was entering through a coastal forest near the Black Sea. The train was coming in quick as one of the Golems, misjudging its angle of attack, crashed. Remains of the Golem littered the land in front of the train as the second patrol shot its cannon at the train.

There was a noise, a crash in the front car of the train. I figured it was just a minor mishap with the engine since it's an old train, so they would have it fixed. But this time, the electricity inside the train went out and the train shook.

I looked out the window, and I saw fire on the side of the train. I knew that it could have been a problem with an engine, but as I looked out the window, I saw a huge fireball hurdling towards our window. That was no engine problem. I sprinted as fast as I could to Amber, my only thought to protect her, and I screamed, "Get Down!"

I duck her down, my body over hers, as the fireball went through the windows. After it passed I took off to check if Pooja and Tommy were okay. I found them coming to me.

"Surya, what's going on?" Pooja asked me, frantic.

I felt fear welling inside me. I checked out the window to see heavy robots outside the train. Golems. Equipped with Machine Guns, one robot shot at the train's wheels, as a second robot shot a fireball at the front of the car. I snarled and told Pooja and Tommy firmly, "It's Laroche's men! You stay right here with Tommy. I'll get Amber."

I ran to the section Amber was in. "Amber, go with Tommy and Pooja. I'll find a way to kill those behemoths!"

I took my bow and arrows, and I jumped from the train. I escaped as another fireball erupted into the train. Right where Amber, Pooja, and Tommy, were. The train scattered under the force of the impact.

I went hustling to the remains of the train. There were body parts all over the site and dead bodies everywhere. I saw no survivors. Emotion overwhelmed me. "Damn it," I whispered.

I started, mourning the loss of my sister and my friends. I fell on my knees, tears dripping down my face like a waterfall.

As the last tears made their slow trail down my cheek, I heard a voice from the distance. My name, being called to me over and over. I recognized that voice. I had heard it in my life and in my dreams. I figured I was crazy with grief, or the fumes of the burnt train remains were getting to me, but as I looked around me, I saw a silhouette. Three of them. I ran to them as their silhouettes came closer.

Finally, I saw them, coughing in the smoke. I felt like I was about to cry again when I saw Amber, Pooja, and Tommy alive.

"Surya, we're so sorry. Were you worried?" Amber stuttered as she embraced me.

I hugged both Amber and Pooja so tight that they almost passed out. After I came back to myself, I put my mind back to our task.

"Well, we're not getting there anytime soon. We might as well hit the road," Pooja said.

"Pooja, are you joking?" I asked her in disbelief. "We are not going out of this forest until I eliminate those Golems. Those monstrous robots out there destroyed this train, with barely an effort. We can't let them loose to kill anyone else."

Tommy wandered around until he found something strange. "Guys, look at these."

I examined the objects very thoroughly until I figured out. They were the remains of Robot Golems. But their hands had been ripped off by something. They lay on the ground. And gave me an idea. "We could use its hands to defend ourselves."

"Good thinking," Tommy said with a smile.

I grabbed the machine gun hand and Tommy grabs the fireball cannon, and we started making our way through the forest in search of any shelter

Chapter VI
Motorcycle Mischief

"Mischief springs from the power which the moneyed interest derives from a paper currency which they are able to control, from the multitude of corporations with exclusive privileges which are employed altogether for their benefit."

-Andrew Jackson

Two days had passed and most of the patrols had been terminated, but since the forest extends through a large area, it took us a very long time to make our way. Tommy got sick due to the immense heat in the forest. Pooja tried to heal Tommy but since he didn't have a strong immune system, it was not working. He didn't eat anything and we had to get him to a hospital immediately. Since Amber was an expert hunter just like me, she hunted a few deer so Pooja could cook as our trip to Istanbul might take at least to two and a half hours.

I, on the other hand attempted to build transportation for us by using the remaining pieces of the train. I found the items I needed, such as the GPS and the hologram map, but didn't find anything to actually power it up. The engine was busted and the wheels were cracked. I had to cobble wheels together to move the chariot. I thought maybe I could find more parts deep in the forest. Something that would help us reach our destination. I went deep in as I tried to find any robots that might power up the chariot.

I went deep enough that I found the route that would take us to Istanbul. The view of the route made my body heat up with rage. It was all destroyed, with burnt sand and palm trees. This path was a ruin, with remains of cars, and robot parts.

It was called Route XI, the pathway traders from 2010 to 2019 used to trade goods from the city of Sofia, Istanbul, or from other European port cities. After the Invasion, the route grew older and fell into disrepair, as many people couldn't take it because of Laroche's men that patrolled the area. Anything that came near the patrols was eliminated. And these robots weren't the only one that patrolled the area. Tommy informed me about the other kinds of patrol that roamed around Route XI. They were called Robo-Scramblers. They look like a motorcycle but can transform into a deadly robot that cannot be annihilated, unless the victim finds its vulnerable spot. Usually, Scramblers are equipped with machine guns on both side, but if threatened, they will transform into a trooper with more speed than a Maglev. Each Robo-Scrambler is equipped with special armor on the inside.

And as I stood there watching, a Scrambler came into view on the pathway.

I saw a motorcycle riding without a person riding it. This was my chance to set up a trap to hack the control pad inside the robot. I didn't have any plan to break its speed. I try to improvise by planting my machine gun arm on the car and connecting wires to it, hopefully to make it fire faster than the Scrambler could move. I had an extra sensor that I could hook to the machine gun. If it sensed the patrol, it would blind it and injure it, allowing me a chance to get at it and access its control pad.

The Robo-Scrambler was coming in fast. As

it reached the point where the gun was, I managed to get a few shots off but the vehicle transformed, sensing the danger, and my improvised weapon missed it.

After it had transformed, it scanned me. I knew what that meant. It knew I was there. So now it was trying to kill me. The Robo-Scrambler was a dark colored motorcycle built to resemble a 1930 Indian Motorcycle. One of my favorites. I could see Laroche's hand in the design. He had my thoughts and my memories.

It transformed into a dark figure and pulled out a double barrelled shotgun, and shot at me, but fortunately missed. With my bow and arrow I got off a lucky shot and took it in its wheel leg. The injury triggered the dark trooper to transform back into the motorcycle form.

The robot was stuck in its motorcycle form, struggling to get back in its humanoid form. I hustled to it, rushing to make sure it couldn't. I grabbed my knife out of my boot and stabbed the motorcycle's wheel, puncturing it, taking away its ability to drive away.

Taking its shotgun away I shot its core open

to find the control system. I examined it, understanding its beautiful simplicity. It was a touch screen with thirteen different controls. Each control had a special job, such on enabling its machine guns or turning sides. I immediately had a thought. I turned on the positive control and all of a sudden, the robot stopped moving.

As I turned off the Notrax mode, its eye turned blue and it was able to change back to its robot mode. It got up. It was under my control now. But then another thought hit me. I may not be able to find a working engine, but I already had a machine that was operating perfectly fine. I could hook the motorcycle up to the vehicle I was constructing.

I operated the motorcycle and drove it to the campsite. As I was riding, the Robo-Scrambler's sensors spotted a Robot Golem just as the monstrous robot spotted me and attempted to terminate me with its machine gun. Using the control pad, I had the Robo-Scrambler eliminate the patrol, using its light shotgun to take out its eye, and then wrap its arms around the head of the Golem and ripping its head off. It went lifeless.

"Do you think you could attach yourself to our vehicle?" I asked the Robo-Scrambler.

"I don't see why not," it answered in a docile, inhuman voice.

Chapter VII
The Arrival

"The Slave Trade, though nominally abolished, is actively pursued here, eighty-three slaves having been landed just before my arrival, and another cargo during my stay."
  -George Gray

The Robo-Scrambler took us all the way to the great port city of Istanbul. But it didn't look so great to us. It looked pitiful and I knew I had to do something. It looked so awful, the way the people were suffering from the damages, the lack of water, and a virtual river of blood from all the dead people. All the corpses were being wrapped for disposal. I saw robots on the ground that were on fire and some were burnt but still moving. It was like the place of torment. I was examining the city, trying to look for any evidence that could lead me to the invaders of this city. But all I could find was this piece of black hair.

Hair. I didn't know what to make of it. This could lead me to the person who was part of the invasion, or to someone who was just trying to defend the city. The hair was a long strand and it looked like it came from a Lion's mane. Possibly a black one. If I was at a laboratory that could read DNA, I could possibly figure out who or what it came from. Where did it come from, how did it transform, and the most important question, why did it come here? These were all questions that needed to be answered.

But whatever it had come from, one thing was obvious from the debris everywhere. That thing did take out many of these robots, maybe all of them, judging by the claw marks sunk deep into their metal skin. But alas, not before they had done a great amount of damage to the city.

Just looking at the marketplace made me realize that this might have been a trap. Laroche might have faked this entire scene to lead me here. I went through the marketplace, ignoring the damages and the tragic scene of the dead people everywhere. Some civilians had damaged faces, others were missing a body part or were severely injured in some other way. I also saw tons of bones with burnt marks on them, skulls broken, their jaws gone. Laroche is truly indeed a terrorist. Until that moment, I had tried to convince myself differently. I could no longer pretend.

As we entered the door of the Grand Palace, I saw the Sultan was waiting by his throne, deep in serious thought. As he stood up to check who was at the door, he cowered in fright. He looked like a dwarf. There were dried blood stains all over his white tunic. He wore a purple turban that had small pearls around it and had a large ruby in the center of it.

We walked up the hall as two guards stopped me by crossing both of their spears together in our path. Scared, Amber grabbed onto my hands tightly.

Something tells me that the Sultan wasn't in a good mood. As he walked to meet me, his fat body waddled and his legs don't even show under his clothes. When he came close to me, I could see the tunic had sweat stains and he was scared to death. "May Allah protect you my son. Laroche is a demon, Surya, that robot! And look what he did to my commander and my right hand man!" Tears started flowing down his cheeks.

The man he pointed to was in pain. He had lost an arm and half of his face was burned off. "Shiva Shiva Shankara, Hara Hara Mahadev," I whisper to myself as I see the soldier in pain. It was tragic to see him suffering. Not only him, but the civilians dying and suffering from pain outside the palace as well. Innocent children who had watched their mother or father die. Amber was crying as she hugged me.

"Prince," the Sultan's wounded commander said to me, "you must avenge my death by killing that monster. I am Hindu, but I came to fight for world peace. When the war between the robots and humans started, I decided to fight. Now, I want to protect my family and avenge the families who died in this invasion. May peace be with you, Prince!" He was coughing blood between sentences. And then, as he said his last words, he died with his eyes open.

"Hey, speak to me. Speak, damn it!" I yelled. But it didn't matter. I couldn't bring him back to life.

The old soldier's death saddened my crew and the Sultan. Pooja tried to keep herself together, but failed as she was crying hard. Tommy tried to comfort her, but nothing he did helped. "I'll put her in her room," he told us, walking away with her.

"Assist the body to the Feriköy Latin Catholic Cemetery and cremate him there," the Sultan ordered his men. "He shall rest in peace."

I waited for the Sultan's men to obey and then I showed him the long strand of black hair. "Sultan, if you have a laboratory here, do you think Tommy could borrow it for two weeks or so? I need it for him to scan this strand of hair."

"I don't see why not," he answered, seeming to feel a little better. "By the way, the Captain of the U.S. Marines told me to assign you your first mission tomorrow. So do whatever you can today. My Advisor has picked out a room for you to stay in, so make yourselves feel at home."

"One question," I said to him, "how long is the Topkapi Palace open till?

Chapter VIII
The Gifts

"All things will be produced in superior quantity and quality, and with greater ease, when each man works at a single occupation, in accordance with his natural gifts, and at the right moment, without meddling with anything else."
-Plato

Night fell. Everyone was asleep. Everyone, that is, except me. I thought about today and everything I had seen in the aftermath of the invasion in the city. It was like the Rwandan Genocide all over again.

I had nothing but a bow with arrows, my Urumi and my flintlock revolver with me. I didn't think I needed any more weapons for now. My Urumi was rusted but still strong enough to tear flesh. It was as flexible as a snake's backbone. As my memories came to me while touching the weapons, I shed tears.

The time was 11:00 PM. I was resting on my bed, thinking about the trouble I had created ever since that damn robot was born. Nothing had been right ever since we had arrived at Istanbul. But there was one question that was foremost in my mind, and I still hadn't gotten an answer.

What do we do now?

As I was thinking, Tommy barged in through the door. "Surya, come quick, I want to show you something."

I followed his trail all the way to the training grounds to the target range section. Tommy lay out a few objects on a table that resembled weapons to me. "Surya, these are what will help you lead Istanbul to freedom. These are high tech military weapons, tested in labs to great effect."

On the table, I saw a light brown fedora, an Indian Talwar, a 9mm pistol, and a double barrelled shotgun. "I built some of these weapons such as the pistol, to act differently from its original design," he explained to me.

I held the pistol, and observed its form and its design. Tommy described it to me. "This is a double barrelled pistol, which is powerful enough to kill a person, maybe even a bear." The pistol was a bronze color with a black handle as strong as the bone of a buck. It felt rough, like the skin of an alligator as I wiped my fingertips slowly against the handle. "Care to shoot it, Surya?"

I grasped onto the handle and aimed at the red and white target at the furthest end of the firing range. I had that same feeling as I did when I was hunting deer in the forest. I closed my eyes and relaxed into the shot as my finger pulled the trigger. I could barely feel the gun kick. As soon as I opened my eyes, I saw two holes dead center of the target.

"Wow, you sure are a 'Bullseye Mcshooter pants', aren't you?" Tommy said.

I went inside with Tommy, complimenting him on how well the pistol shoots. I stopped when I see a fine looking suit of armor. I walked over to the armor, admiring its craftsmanship and the feel of it. It consisted of a black short-sleeved pullover jacket. Instead of a helmet it sported a brown fedora with no design that had that ancient feeling when I brushed the flat surface of the brim.

On the arms of the mannequin were gauntlets that looked dangerous even to me. Tommy removed them off the hands and placed them on my wrists. "These are military grade weapons. Use them responsibly, no damage. Use them poorly, boatloads of damage. They're filled with weapons such as a hidden blade, poison darts, and a rope dart. Not to mention three smoke grenades. The second gauntlet holds your tools, such as the computer virus flash-drive, a map, and a hologram communicator. Each gauntlet is equipped with a rope dart, so you'll be swinging like Tarzan,"

As the gauntlets tighten, they stab my wrists with a little needle built into both gauntlets. "That's their way of sensing their new owner," Tommy explained. "They take a sample of your blood, scans it, and finally it permanently locks onto to you. If someone tried to steal them, there will be no chance of them trying to access the weapons."

"Scanning person's bio," said the smooth voice of the onboard gauntlet computer. "Hello, Suryadeva. Your age is twenty-one, your height is six feet and one inch, your weight is one hundred and sixty pounds, and your blood type is positive A. Is this correct?"

I pressed the Yes button on the touchpad

and view all the option for me to select.

"Well, it seems like you've gotten the hang of the concept," Tommy said. "Now, time for your hat."

He placed the fedora on my head. It felt heavy and bulky. "This is an electronic fedora. It doesn't stab you with the needle like the gauntlets did, but it will scan your brain by gripping itself onto your head. So, it's going to lock onto you, and you will have the power to enhance the experience. If you press the HEV button, that enables your vision to become sharper to view your enemies or to find things around the environment. Just put the jacket and everything else on, and see how it works tomorrow. If it is fine, you'll be assigned to your first mission tomorrow."

"Very good, Tommy. I'm impressed with the way you built it for me." I compliment him as he put them away again.

"Hey," he said, "anything for my best childhood friend."

"All right, thanks man. Tomorrow, we got a big day ahead of us. We have to go to the Grand Library of Topkapi."

Sultanahmet District
Istanbul, Turkey

Chapter IX
The Library

"Learning is the discovery that something is possible"
 -Fritz Perls

I felt weird inside my body. I wasn't used to having a schedule I had to follow now. I couldn't even do the things I normally did during the day. Like hunt. I couldn't hunt due to the lack of forests in Istanbul.

Not that it mattered. Today was the day Tommy and I were going to the Topkapi Palace to search the information at the library there. The old lady had told me this, that I would find the means to lead this country to its independence from the Notrax's rule.

Open the   doo s of the east
a you sh ll find sec t that have not been
reveale for mill nia

The odd inscription on the parchment given to me by the old lady, once I had deciphered it, said to open the doors of the east. The east meant the east wing of the palace and according to the map of the Topkapi Palace, there was only one room in the east wing. The Grand Library of Turkey, holding its information from the beginning of life to the findings of Piri Reis, an Ottoman explorer.

After Tommy had presented the equipment to me, I decided to start the journey off with decrypting the parchment further to understand what part of the library I should go to in order to. As we went out the door, Tommy got on a motorcycle and put his shotgun in the black leather holster.

"Let's take the horses," I suggested. "It'd be easier. The museum closes at five o'clock for a dinner break. It's now four thirty."

He shrugged and got off the motorcycle again. "Fine."

As soon as we got there, I noticed how there were no people around the entrance. It seemed like the rush to see the palace was already over. I touched the sides of the entry hall and felt how they had the same feel to them as my hat did when I brushed its material.

"We should go to the second courtyard, that's where the library may be," I said to Tommy. "But we have to hurry up. The library will close and I can't come back today because Amber and I have a dinner to go to, and then I'm assigned a mission. My day is filled and this is my only day I can spare to find secrets in this library that may help us."

After going through the courtyards and finding the doors of the east, we found that there was no library here after all. Tommy and I split up to check the east wings of each courtyard, but didn't find anything resembling a library holding the secrets of this country.

"Are you sure that old hag said that there was a library here?" Tommy asked me. "I mean come on, we checked each courtyard but still we didn't find any library here, Surya."

Disheartened, I checked the parchment again. "Wait, this inscription has an empty space," I discovered.

"So? What does it matter?"

"Because it looks like it was smeared or erased. Let me try the HEV, then I could figure out what the word might have been. I bet we'd be able to figure out where in this palace the library is then."

I pressed the button on my hat that activated the enhancement for my eyes to locate what I was looking for. But when I did, I fell to the ground in intense pain as if my eyes were melting. I groaned and twisted with the pain. After what seemed like hours but was actually probably more like thirty seconds the pain started to fade away.

Opening my eyes I saw green everywhere. Looking at Tommy, I saw him silhouetted in red with a clear indication that he was equipped with a revolver on his side.

"Surya, are you all right?" the Tommy silhouette asked me.

"Yeah, what happened?"

"I should have warned you. This is the HEV. This is what helps you finish your objectives. It connects with your brain, and it causes your eyes to feel pain as it changes your vision. It reads the thoughts in your head and uses those thoughts to lead you to your final point on your mission."

"Well, how do I find out what my enemies are wielding? Like that revolver you have there?"

"That's easy. If they're holding a firearm, such as a pistol or a long gun, then they are highlighted as red, informing you that they are dangerous and hard to eliminate. If they are highlighted as orange, they are equipped with a bladed weapon. If the enemy is highlighted as blue, they are not armed nor equipped with any kind of weapon, but the color changes as the threat changes. They can turn green when nervous or threatened and then finally turn red or orange if there is a arsenal near them. Possibly if there is a box with a gun inside of it, but I doubt you will encounter something like that."

"All right, thanks for explaining." I took a glance of the parchment as my vision started scanning its smeared words. When it reached one hundred percent to get the accurate results, the missing word appeared in the picture, showing the correct inscription before it had been erased:

Open the hidden doors to the East of the park of the Sultans, and you shall reveal secrets for the millennia

"Tommy, this inscription says 'the hidden doors to the East of the park of the Sultans.' That means that in one of these courtyards in the east section, there might be an open door to the library!" I exclaimed, reflecting on my previous mistake.

"But it doesn't tell us which courtyard," Tommy pointed out, "so how are we going to figure out which one holds the trigger to the doors?"

I was trying to figure out the answer to that problem when the light bulb went off in my head. "If we don't know which courtyard to check, then why don't we use the HEV button?"

Tommy's face brightened. "Do you know how to transfer the map to your hat?"

"Uh, no, why?"

"If we could transfer the map over to your hat, then we could access many things inside the palace. Here, just press the transfer application on your gauntlet and type in Topkapi overview map."

I opened up the latch on the gauntlet and pressed the transfer application. "Are you sure you want to transfer the Topkapi Palace overview map to the destination Fedora Hat?" that smooth computer voice asked me.

I pressed the yes button on my touch pad and it started to transfer the map to the hat. The wireless connection here must be good, because as soon as I pressed the button that transferred the map, it was done in less than five seconds. "Okay," I said, "so now the map is in that hat and I can view it, what should I do next?"

Tommy had a relieved look on his face after he found out the map was successfully transferred onto my hat. "Now that it has been transferred, you think of your objective, and the hat will read it, linking it with the map and finally allowing you to find the location you need on the map. Now, just relax and allow your hat to do all the work."

I relaxed for a moment, just thinking of what makes me happy, reaching my focus. Little did I know the mental pictures I was using to focus my mind were being transferred onto Tommy's computer and he was secretly looking at them. I was thinking of Amber, the most important women in my life. I thought of her as her hair was blowing in the wind, and the lasting memories I had collected of her. The day she said "I love you" before she left Abgabeschule in tears. I made sure that Shiva, my guardian god, not only protected Pooja and me, but protected her for eternity. Now, later in life, he answered my pleas to protect her by bringing us together so I could do exactly that. I decided it was time I decided to tell Amber how I really felt about her, about my crush on her and my renewed love.

I opened my eyes up to find the hat was showing the location of the hidden library in the third courtyard near the hollow tree. It showed where the switch was inside the tree. The hat showed me the hidden mechanism which was nothing but a weight system. Once a person got inside of it, it would transport them down, acting like an elevator.

"Tommy, head to the third courtyard to the hollow fig tree. Get inside now, we have no time to waste!" I rushed him as fast as possible because I was going to be late for my dinner with Amber.

The mechanism in the hidden tree worked just like the hat had described it would. After we had been transported to the hidden library of the Topkapi Palace, I stopped for just a brief moment to take in the impressive sight. I saw so many shelves, filled with many secrets.

The room was a dark room with no electricity or air conditioning. There were books about secret topics such as the Darklands of the Anatolian Plateau and the mythical creatures of Zonguldak. There were other secret books as well. I could spend a lifetime here and be happy doing so. But what we really needed was the diary of Piri Reis in which he revealed many secrets like the mysterious Mystique ship that crashed on Socotra before his death. But the diary was hidden. It was nowhere to be found.

Until Tommy found something.

"Hey, Surya!" he said. "Look what I found!"

Turns out he had found a dial in which turning numbers unlocked a door. As I scanned the inside of the room with the HEV in my hat, I saw a book was hidden inside. It was the diary of

Piri Reis. I could see all of the pages. From treasures to lost civilizations, this book had everything, all of the secrets ever recorded by him. I wondered why he hid it.

"Wait, this dial is four numbers. What do you think could unlock the door?" I asked. The lock could be unlocked only by a four digit number. Which gave us 10,000 possible combinations to choose from.

"Do you think it could be his birth year?" Tommy asked. I had to agree that was a possibility. But he had been born between the year 1465 and 1470. I didn't know what his actual birth year was. No one did. But I tried entering each of those numbers in, to no effect.

There was one other date that was very specific. "What if he entered the year of his death? It's possible that it could be the right code." I entered in 1553, the year of his death. Then, we heard the sharp sound of something opening. I was certain that a latch must have opened. Sure enough, when I tried the door it gave easily and opened up to me.

I saw something in the ground, covered with

cobwebs and dust. It was a stone pillar that held the diary up from the ground.

"Tommy, look at this," the stone pillar had ancient inscriptions on the side of it. It was about waist high, and the pillar was all covered in dried blood. "His diary. Piri Reis' diary. Every secret that Istanbul has was revealed inside his diary. Everything." I spoke in amazement as I looked through the pages, observing the quality of the book, the detail of the sketches, the wealth of information. The diary was a brown book full of faded pages. As I read each page, it came to me that someone had tried to burn the book sometime in the distant past. Scorch marks discolored many of the pages. Drawings, diagrams, entries, everything was in that book.

"All right then," I remarked, happy this part of our journey was complete. "Let's just bring this to the Grand Palace and we'll read it there."

Chapter X
Crash landing

"I shot down some German planes and I got shot down myself, crashing in a burst of flames and crawling out, getting rescued by brave soldier."
    -Roald Dahl

My first mission was assigned by the Sultan. He wanted me to bring the battle plans Laroche had stored inside his computer at Jeddah back to him for analysis. People have been saying that near the eastern shore of Saudi Arabia, only twenty miles away from Mecca, there was an abandoned mosque, and the computer was put there for shelter. But after the invasion was over, Laroche and his hordes had wiped the Arabian Peninsula clean. No humans, nothing. The Notrax took the mosque after they had killed the people, and made it their military base. That's where they keep the robotic animals, such as the Sabretooths, and vipers, and cobras. They store weapons there of all different kinds. Even Navy Seals tried to enter the mosque but all of them were exterminated. The entire Middle East was wiped out. The Muslims were put in shelters near Indonesia, because Laroche wanted to make the Muslim people his slaves. That's how great his hatred of me and my people had become.

So the United States government decided to evacuate every single person in the Middle East except the people ruling the Middle East countries, and the ones fighting for the Middle East. That was fine for those who valued their lives and wanted to keep living. Well, guess what? Sultan Byziwad sent me on a mission to go to the eastern coast of Saudi Arabia. Why?

Here's how it all started. It was the day I had returned from our anniversary dinner with Amber. After hearing about the mishap that happened at the restaurant, the Sultan began to question our loyalty and suspect we had plans of our own. So Sultan Byziwad, who had tried sending many people to Saudi Arabia only to see them killed, thought I would be the logical choice to go next. For his own reasons.

"Surya," he said to me, all smiles and tender

grace, "I need to talk to you about something. Can you come in my office?"

I was terrified. Was he going to designate me as one of his generals? Or maybe something else? My friends were all nudging me to go and meet with him.

Easy for them. They didn't have to go.

"Surya, so the reason I wanted you to come meet with me is that there is a mosque near Jeddah, only about just three miles away,"

"Yeah, and there is something you need from it?"

He nodded. "Somehow, none of our spies came back, so I'm sending you. This is a very important job. All I need you to do is just spy on the army, just see what they're doing. Oh. Well. Another thing, we've given you a helicopter, a rifle, plus I have given you a pistol. I need you to kill the guards. Then after all the guards have been killed, I need to you copy some documents onto this." He handed me a small device. It was a black and portable hard drive that was about the size of my fist.

"You must take Laroche's plans that are in

the mosque. Thomas has already transferred the overview and 3-D map of the mosque into your gauntlet."

I opened the map on my gauntlet and took a look at the map. Sultan Byziwad pointed on the map. "This here is the entrance. Don't come through here. My men have told me that the guards at all of the entrances are heavily armored. The last thing I need is another dead man. Remember, Zahaar is in charge and will alert the rest if one guard dies. It would be a good idea to attack from above. Now the courtyard is the entrance to the area that has the plans, which is the prayer room. You get in the prayer room, which is where the plans are, and once you get the plans, get out of the mosque. I will make arrangements to send a helicopter to retrieve you.

"All right. Well the journey starts in two days so pack everything you need. I have made arrangements to send a cargo plane to take you to Jeddah."

Wait. Did he say cargo plane?

"Do you mean cargo as in trucks, cars, explosives?"

You know what he said?

"Of course."

I thought he was going to just send me on a mission.

"But what is all that for?"

"After the mission we have to bomb the mosque," he said with a shrug. "It's nothing personal. It's just that we need to destroy those mechanical animals in there. There are no more religious things in there. It is a dead place."

It made perfect sense that he was going to bomb the mosque, when he put it that way.

So then it started. I spent the next two days getting ready for the trip. Two days later, I started to pack up for the trip. There were marines getting ready for me, actual marines that went out of the Turkish country. They were strong, tough, and they carried huge guns such as the PKM LMG. There were U.S. Marines, too. Some, such as the gas mask marines, were wielding M32 grenade launchers. Others such as wore a bandana around their mouth and they wore sunglasses to protect their eyes from the sand. They also wore heavy armor, and they were wielding a SPAS-12 or M4 assault rifles.

The plane was full of soldiers. Pirates that had just joined the team, Navy Seals with their high tech gadgetry, and the black operation team that also joined the marines.

After the conquest of the Middle East, Laroche stole cannons from the time period of the revolutionary war, and howitzer cannons. He camouflaged them and hid them around the deserts of the Middle East, waiting for any military planes that might come nearby. No one has ever seen these cannons because they are so well blended in with the desert environment. But now Laroche brought them to bear and eliminated the nearby planes, because back at the mosque, they knew that Surya was approaching the Syrian desert.

They had a radar showing them any activity going on. After one of the androids found us on the radar, he reported to the General in command of the mosque, General Zahaar. "General, there's some plane activity going on. Should we alert the cannon team?"

Zahaar looked irritated as he said, "Lock and load." The team was alerted immediately, and they prepared to fire the cannons.

I was in Syria, right near Homs just about five miles away from the city. It was barren, no sign of civilization, nothing. Everything was gone just like so much of my beloved land, reduced to sand, and broken towers, buildings, citadels, and fortresses. As I sat watching the city, I saw something move, like a long stick with a hole at its spout. I had a bad feeling about it. Then finally I figured out what that stick was.

"Everybody duck!" I yelled. It was a cannon, maybe a howitzer. It shot a fireball at the plane, rocking us, sending many of us flying out of our seats. As I got up, the plane was on fire. A gaping hole had been shot open at the side of the plane. Everything was falling out. Equipment, parts of planes, even soldiers. Then another missile hit us on the other side of the plane. The plane was being torn in half, and our only chance of survival was to abandon it. So I jumped while I still had the chance.

The plane finally exploded high above me, the sound of it deafening. I knew a moment of panic when I thought I would die, before I took control of myself and shot my chained hook. It caught on a load of falling cargo. I retracted the hook, slamming myself against the boxes in mid-air. I had to get the parachute opened. I reached for it, to find it was just out of my grasp.

But then I knew what to do in a flash. I extended the concealed rope knife in the gauntlet and cut the cord securing the parachute. It released, catching the air, slowing our descent, letting me live.

After I landed, I thought I should go back to the plane and check on the others. I did. But I regretted it. It turned out I was the only survivor in the crash. The Marines, the soldiers, all of them, were sunk into the sand as it burned around them. The snout of the plane stuck out in the middle of the carnage. It was a sandy graveyard. Every single person on the plane died. Everybody except me.

"You've got to be kidding me!" I muttered to myself. I would have to walk from here. Homs was near the border of Lebanon. I had a long way to go.

"Sir, the plane is down," the android said to his General.

"You know that was the plane our target was on."

The troop that gave the status report was confused. "Well, we have tons of targets, but which one?"

"The one who built Laroche. You know Suryadeva, the hero, the one going out for revenge. God, I don't know why Laroche built you stupid robots. I feel like I'm the smartest one here."

After the fall of the plane, Laroche made a video call. "Well, what progress do we have? Are there any survivors left in the Middle East?"

"There are a few," the android reported. "Over 20,000 people are in Mecca right now at Masjid al-Haram, the largest mosque in the world. We tried attacking them but there is some threat that is attacking us. There's no way that we can wipe out the population. It's too dangerous even for us."

"We can't wipe them out. This threat to us is very dangerous. Plus, all the Muslims have traveled to Indonesia. It's pointless just to migrate over there and attack. At least we're about to conquer Istanbul. Once I have taken over the throne, I can treat all the humans like slaves. They will pay for treating robots like dogs."

"Don't get your hopes up too high, brother." Zahaar mutters to himself and chuckles softly.

Laroche was confused for a while. "Why do you say that? I mean nothing can threaten us. I gave Byziwad the warning."

"Well, I have observed on the cannon-cam that Surya, your creator and our greatest foe, has been observing the scene of the city of Homs, and I saw him on the plane when the missile hit it."

"First, he's not my creator! And the Sultan told me that he wouldn't come otherwise, I would murder him if he called any help to come here. That meant the Prince, too!" Laroche did not believe the Sultan would dare go against him.

"If you don't believe me, check out the cam yourself."

Laroche did. He scanned the whole area with the cam really good, and still didn't see him there. But the second part of the video showed a clear picture of him on that plane. Laroche boiled with anger, and acidic juices in his internal mechanisms spouted up into his mouth. He knew that there had to be serious consequences for Istanbul.

"Call the Special Operation team," he ordered. "Tell them to kidnap the Sultan and the President's daughter. Now."

I was all alone, hoping for a miracle to happen, but I just kept on walking. I collapsed to the ground a few times when my legs gave out.

The night was coming on quickly. I couldn't find an oasis to rest for the night nor a camel to cut open for an emergency shelter. I would freeze to death if I didn't find shelter. As dusk faded away, the night began. In the Syrian desert, my body had burned all day. Now, it would freeze. I was beginning to become sick from the harsh extremes.

Fifteen hours later, it was dawn. Sick as I was I just kept on walking. I was searching everywhere looking for an oasis, when all of a sudden I saw something. Something that was not a hallucination.

Chapter XI
Kraks des Chevaliers

"The object of life is not to be on the side of the majority, but to escape finding oneself at the ranks of the insane."
   -Marcus Aurelius

Back at the palace, Sultan Byziwad made Thomas contact me. Using the long-range communication gear in Surya's gauntlets, he was able to contact him easily. "Surya, are you okay? Where the hell are you?"

"The plane crashed and exploded," I answered, my stomach twisting and my throat dry as dust. I was in pain. "Laroche's men have been alerted, because the plane crashed because of a Notrax cannon, I think maybe two. They know I'm coming and they will come for the Sultan to attack him. You must protect him at all costs. God, it's so hot! I've been walking day and night, and I think I may be sick."

I lost my voice. I didn't think I could go on.

"Do you want to cancel the mission, Surya?"

Tommy recommended, seeing how bad my health was.

"I will continue this mission," I told him. "I'll make sure you get those plans. All I need is water and some time to heal myself up, but it seems like there are no oases around the Syrian. This is definitely not the Sahara desert. Could take me weeks to get around the entire desert, maybe even months."

Amber heard me talking, and came as quickly as possible. "Surya, where are you?" she said frantically. "I've been so worried about you, I couldn't sleep!"

"I'm coming, Amber. I'll make it back, I promise. But now, I need you not to worry about me. Make sure Pooja takes her light seeds."

Amber loved Surya from the day she met him. Now, here is how it all started.

Amber came to Berlin fifteen years ago. Her parents were in the middle of a crisis, and for them that actually meant war. So for her safety, they sent her off to Berlin, thinking she would be safe in a school called Abgabeschule, the school for

Royals. Surya was there too. He wasn't very popular. He wasn't athletic. He was smart, kind, and very strong. But none of his peers admired him for these qualities. All they saw, was his freakish intelligence. He was shy, and he was considered pathetic by most.

He had always loved Amber, from the moment he laid eyes on her. He had known her ever since the day when the U.S. and India had become friends. She was very pretty, smart, not very athletic, but a great gunner as it turned out.

When she first came to that school, she didn't know Surya even though her parents and his parents were friends.

Now Amber was dating Peter, the British prince. He wore Vans shoes, grey skinny jeans, and he wore a british polo shirt most every day. He played on the Major League Soccer team for London, and was known as the youngest soccer player in the world. Surya's idea of sports involved archery, and sword-fighting, horse riding, gun range practice. But he never told anyone that. In fact, his entire life was a secret.

One day, Surya was reading while walking to

his class, and Amber was texting while walking to class, and both of them bumped into each other.

"I'm sorry, I'm sorry," they both laughed. It felt like love at first sight for each of them when both of them locked eyes with each other. She had the perfect indigo colored eyes, and he had brown eyes that shined in the sun.

To Amber, Surya had the kind of strength that a woman valued in a man. She knew his heart instantly. His hair was a deep shade of black that drew her eyes. There was something about him that made her think, wow.

So ever since that day, Surya and Amber started hanging out with each other, which aggravated Peter. He got jealous when Surya and Amber were walking down the science department hallway. One day, Surya was walking Amber to her class, and Peter came in. "What'cha doin' with my girlfriend, idiot?" he said with a snarl.

"Oh, I'm sorry. I didn't mean to cause any trouble." Surya said, shyly smiling.

"Well, the only way I will accept your apology is if I rearrange your face," was Peter's response. Peter threw his fist at Surya.

Surya dodged it. It hit the locker. Surya heard the small bones in Peter's hand snap. He was in agony. Everybody gasped. No one had ever been able to dodge Peter before. And now, Surya had?

Surya was horrified at all of the attention. He kept apologizing over and over as he ran away.

Not long after that happened, Surya was cornered by three of Peter's friends, along with Peter. He might have been able to defend himself. If he was that kind of person. Instead, he got beat so bad he was coughing blood.

"Ain't so tough now, are you?" Peter laughed at him.

And that was all it took. Surya stood up, and punched Peter squarely in his gut. He was shocked. He punched back at Surya but he dodged it and landed more punches at Peter. Peter's friends stepped in, taking Surya off Peter, allowing Peter to land more punches on Surya.

And that was when Amber came in with some of her friends. She was horrified at what Peter and his friends were doing. "Why are you beating him up?" she demanded.

"That idiot deserves some real punches, chasing us british out, and dating my girlfriend!"

"Your girlfriend?" she asked, her eyebrows raised. "Uh...I don't think so. Why would you hurt him? From, now on, we are no longer together. I would rather date him than date you. We're through!"

Peter was so shocked. In fact, he was embarrassed that she broke up with him so publicly like that. For Surya? He couldn't accept it.

When he was at lunch, she hung out with Surya. Surya didn't believe her that she was dating him. No one ever dated him. Especially someone like Amber. She was the prettiest girl at school. So he stayed her friend, not believing that there could ever be anything between them. It wasn't until they were leaving Abgabeschule permanently that she said, "Surya, you should know that I always liked you. To remember our friendship, I'm giving you this."

She gave Surya a bracelet that had a half heart. "It's been the best time of my life meeting you, and getting to know you. Here is a bracelet for you to remember me. This way, even if I die, I'll still be with you.

Surya had so much he wanted to say, wanted to ask. But there was no time.

"Amber, your ride is here!" the dean of the school yelled across the ocean of kids.

"I got to go." Amber turned to Surya, tears in her eyes, and hugged him tightly.

Then she whispered, "I love you."

She ran off to her ride. Her limo drove away, leaving Surya standing there, wondering what to do. After everyone left, Surya was still there, wondering what he could have done differently, and wondering if he would have a second chance.

Amber still remembered the day she met Surya. Ever since she gave him that bracelet, she had kept the other half of that heart. She made it into a locket, and attached it to her necklace.

In the light of the sun hitting the Syrian desert, I was still stranded alone in the desert. There was no water, no oasis. It was just plain barren. Then I saw something. Something wide, and large. It looked like a city. I rubbed my eyes to see if it was a hallucination, but this time it was real. I ran down the steep slopes of the sand as fast as my legs could go. I kept on falling when I was running. I was so weak. But I couldn't stop myself. I was so anxious to see the city. I wanted water. There must be water here.

I was hearing sounds and thought again I must be dreaming or crazy. It sounded like there was a tavern there. Then I saw something else. There I was, just three feet away from the castle. Right at the corner of my eye, there was a sign. It has dusty, hard to read, but I did my best. It was in Arabic.

Welcome to Kraks de Chevalier
Home to Syria's soldiers

This was Kraks de Chevaliers, the famous crusader fortress in Syria. It was settled by the Kurds after the first crusade. I had read about this bedtime story when I was little. Once upon a time it had been full of tourists, had plant life, and the fortress was colorful. But after the conquest of the Middle East, the fortress fell into ruins.

It was on a large hill. The castle was breaking. It was very fragile. I leaned against a pillar for support only to have it break into millions of pieces.

I tried opening the door, but it was useless. The door was sealed shut. So I had to scan the fortress on the HEV to see if I could find an alternative entrance. I enabled it on my hat, and I could see it in blue everywhere. As I scanned the exterior of the fortress, I saw a yellow triangle indicating a way inside. It was a secret opening in the wall. I ran to it, and had to climb up to it. My limbs were weak, and my head spun, but I did it.

When I got to the other side, I started to climb down, but then the ledges crumbled underneath me, and I fell. My body was sore. It was aching. I felt like my head was going to explode. When I got up, I started walking, not knowing what I was doing or where I was going, and I fell. I kept falling when I hit the ground. That's when I looked up and saw a stream that could have been the water source for all of civilization. There used to be a plumbing system in here, because I saw a broken pipe made out of steel sticking out of the wall. But it looked like it just broke. I followed the trail of the dried stream, and there it was.

It was the most beautiful thing I had ever imagined. It was more precious than gold, more precious than anything else in the world. There on the ground was a puddle of water. It was about three feet wide, and two feet long. And I really didn't care how big it was. It was there. It was pure holiness, just drinking the water off the ground. After I had drank my fill, I stood up and I saw something intriguing. Words on the wall. They were written in dried blood. The blood was brown from age, and it read:

GET AWAY FROM THIS PLACE!
BEWARE OF THE ROBOTS!

There was a hand print in blood, dried and old like the rest of it. Next to the message was a dead husk of a rotting body, being eaten by insects. The body was in black heavy armor. It had the

Navy Seals coat of arms on the armor. Then I realized this body hadn't been here as long as I first thought. It was from the investigations Turkey and the U.S. had sent to the mosque.

As I knelt there processing this, a body dropped on the puddle. A fresh one just killed. It was bleeding and infecting the precious water source.

There was a voice from high above me. Probably the thing that killed this poor man. "That's all of them. Gather some of the troops and send them to Jeddah. Leave the rest here. If you see any humans and they leave out of this death hole, the Captain will execute you once and for all! Do you understand? He's here around the desert. Somewhere. Maybe inside the fortress. The trap has been set up. Soon, we will show the world how worthless humans are after we kill Surya!"

After they had left, I heard the robots gathering in a room nearby. I walked to the room slowly and I saw all the robots gathered together, watching something. I had to get out of there. I turned, running for life.

I saw something move. It was human. At

least, it looked human. I went after it. The struggling, nearly dead man wasn't hard to catch up with. I saw the uniform. A Navy Seal.

"Thank goodness," he said to me. "Finally, another human is here. It's been so long since I met one and had water, food, and I'm stuck here in this godforsaken fortress. Any chance you could get me out of here?"

This man was dying, so all I had to do was what I do best. Improvise.

"All right, but for now, rest. We both need it. In the morning, we'll escape out of here."

I brought us back to the holy pipe where there was so much water still running. The only problem was that I don't how much water there was left.

As night fell outside, I reached out into the pipeline and discovered that there was no more water. From what I knew now about this place, Kraks de Chevaliers was a cruel and harsh environment, filled with danger everywhere.

We had to get out, and this might be our only way. So I went inside the pipe. I barely fit. I had to keep struggling just to move forward. I made it finally to the other end. I fell onto the ground and landed into a puddle. The water was coming from an underground room. It was a large room. The connecting pipe was broken letting some of the water to flow out like a beautiful waterfall. As I was collecting some of the water in my canteen, I saw something. I opened up my HEV on my hat and saw a wooden door hidden behind the waterfall. It was glistening, so there must have been something important inside of here.

Inside the door, I found an arsenal stockpiled by the robots. They have equipped rifles, pistols, snipers, grenades, shotguns, launchers. I figured it was nice of them to leave these things here for me. So I packed all the weapons I could for on my journey, and climbed up the pipe, pushing the weapons ahead of me, as fast as I could while struggling.

The sun started to awaken as the morning arrived. As I came out of the pipe, there were five robots surrounding me. The Navy Seal, the man I thought I was rescuing, was standing with them, a gun in his hand. Probably a .44 caliber derringer.

"What are you doing?" I demanded from him. But I had already guessed.

"There, there, old buddy. At least, I have lived. And look, I have the same kind of weapon that killed President Lincoln, and now I'm going to use it to kill you. Get up here and don't say a word until I contact the Captain," he ordered me as he held the pistol near my heart.

I climbed out of the hole, and put my hands up. "One move, and you die," he said to me. "Captain Laroche will be pleased with the results, soldiers."

As the man looked away from me briefly, I quickly twisted his arm, cracking it. I made a run for it and got to cover. Only then did I realize that I had left my bag of weapons behind.

One of the robots released the mechanical animals to find me. The Smilodon leaped onto the pillar ahead of me, managing to scratch me after I got up there. A huge mark appeared on my leg and blood started flowing out. I tried to injure the beast with my Urumi, but it was no use. It couldn't cut the flesh of its thick armor.

Then, it came to me. As I jumped off the

pillar, I quickly took out my bow and arrow and shot it at the eye of the Smilodon. It cupped its eye, but then started screeching as it began to die. It released large amounts of hydrogen. One louder roar comes out of it and it fell lifeless on the ground as the toxins inside the arrow affected the Smilodon.

The giant robot cobra came charging at me as I rolled out of the way. I took an axe from off the ground, and chopped the head off. The head started rolling halfway across the inner court.

I caught sight of the man who had led me into this trap trying to get away. As he tries to escape, I shot the gauntlet knife at his leg, and it clings onto the ground, making him unable to move. As he was struggling, I come towards him and I want to kill him. I unleash my hidden blade, and put it near his heart. Carefully, I dug the hidden blade deep into his heart. As I took it out, I saw the blood dripping from the blade. It starts pouring out of his mouth. The soldier says one last sentence before he goes to hell. "Laroche will hunt you down and avenge my death."

I stop and pause for a moment. Then I turn

around and say, "I will sacrifice myself for the country, and I will kill that traitor if I have to take ten days or ten years."

One week later
Center of the Rub al
Khali
Arabian Peninsula

Chapter XII
Mecca

"There is no need for temples, no need for complicated philosophies. My brain and my heart are my temples; my philosophy is my kindness."
    -Dalai Lama

It was so bright to be out in the sun again. It was two days since I had gotten out of Kraks de Chevaliers. My god, I prayed fervently. I had survived one night without water. All five bottles were done already. Cleaned out. Every single drop of the precious water I had scrounged from the broken supply pipe. All I could see was hallucinations everywhere in the desert. I fell on to the ground tasting the bitter sand on my tongue and feeling it crust into my eyes and make them burn.

I didn't want to give up but I didn't think I could go on. My eyes started closing. Then, I saw people with ropes tied into a creature's nose. They jumped on this creature with two humps and rode to my body where I lay on the desert floor. That was the last I knew. Then, my eyes closed.

The next thing I knew was cool air all around my body. It felt so soothing after what had felt like an eternity in the desert. Then, I felt a cooler air on my cheek. I heard breathing and a voice right next to me. I opened my eyes just a bit to see a little girl right in front of me. She was speaking in Arabic.

And then another voice said to her, "Go to Mommy in the bazaar, ok sweetheart? Leave the poor man alone."

After she went running out the door, a man walked over to me. I was laying down on a bed, and I sat up. "No, please do not put any stress on yourself," the man said to me.

The man walked over to a container that was gloriously full of water. "Here you are."

Oh my that heavenly goodness. I drank, and drank. Water spilled down my shirt and all over my face. The man sat down and handed me another cup. "Marhaba Sauddi," he said to me.

I didn't understand Arabic more than a few basic phrases. What the man had said went beyond me. He realized my confusion. "English, perhaps?" I nodded, and he smiled. "Pleased to meet you. I think you might have come for the Masjid al- Haram. Although, I did not think I would see an Indian here. Who are you, kind sir?"

He spoke with a heavy Arabic accent. He looked like a poor person judging by his clothes and his house. It looked like an earthquake had come through the area and left its damage behind. Water was leaking from his roof into the bucket in the center of the room. The beds were bunk beds and the sheets were old rags.

"Oh, where are my manners?" the man said into the silence as I tried to work up enough strength to speak. "My name is Ibrahim-Abdul. You may call me Dul. You may think that I am half Jewish and half Muslim, and you're thinking the right way. My mother was Jewish, but my father was Muslim. So that's how it became. And your name is, sir?"

"Surya," I managed at last. "I am the Prince of India."

"Ah, yes, you are the one helping Turkygan."

"I'm sorry, what now?" I didn't know even

that much Arabic.

"Perhaps english?" he said again. "Turkey."

"Yes, I am. But where am I? All I remember was that I passed out in the middle of the desert after I crash landed with my army. To be honest, this place looks suspicious to me. No offense."

He helped me out of the bed and led me out to a place with people in white robes. It was marketplace full of people, and in the back, it had a building that was as big as the Washington memorial. It was the Masjid al Haram. That's when I knew, I was in Mecca.

"Welcome to Mecca, birthplace of Islam."

He said it with much pride. I was so close to Jeddah, so close to my objective. It was a fantastic place to be. I can hear goats bleating near a butcher's market, and see carcasses that smelled like roadkill dead and plucked over by vultures for days on end. When I turned around, I saw Dul had put on white robe with weapons hanging from his body in different spots. "Here, wear this," he said to me.

It was a white jacket that was strikingly similar to my other jacket except it was white. It was mandatory to wear white, he explained to me, because this was a holy place. I was required to follow the Islamic rules here. I kept my hat, however, and Dul gave me my weapons.

"The way this works around in Mecca," Dul explained, "is that we stick together. I am the leader of the Arabian forces. See them right there with the white hooded robes and crossbows behind their back? See their gauntlets that shine? Those are my forces. They will help you find your way out of this place."

"Dul, look at the surroundings. Look at what is happening. There are Notrax troops. They have heavy armor and have surrounded this place. We can't escape out of here. If we could, then how would we do it?

Well, Dul had a plan that was well drawn out. He explained the basics of it to me. "See since today is July Twentieth, the day of Ramadan, the mosque is going to be filled with so many people. They will all be wearing white, and since you have your white on, we will sneak you in the mosque. My men will eliminate the robot troops. When we have eliminated every single one, then we run out of this god forsaken place. Do you hear me?"

As I came out of the shack, I met with Dorgan, the sergeant of the team. He came over and told me that this plan will work out just fine. He took me to the arsenal where the Arabian forces keep their weapons.

So as the afternoon passed and people started to crowd in the mosque, Dul and his men started to scatter around. I jumped up the pillars, and drew my blade. Then the fun began.

I jumped on an android, and stabbed it right in the head. I took out my silenced sniper, and shot a humanoid that was about to shoot one of Dul's men. When I started to climb another pillar, my hand was shot by a sniper bullet.

I fell off the pillar, and I heard the robot send the warning, "Red alert, assassins." That's when the war started.

People were running around like crazy. As for me, I started to throw the guns over to Dul's men. They started shooting at the robots. Dul exclaimed over the shooting, "What's taking so long?!"

"I don't know," I told him, "My gauntlet

went all screwy! It's not showing me any solutions! It's not even working!"

"Use this!" He threw a taser gun in my direction and I caught it from the air. I attached the gun to where it belonged on my gauntlet, and heard that same smooth robotic voice saying "Scanning body. Suryadeva, welcome. Scanning environment. Solutions available."

I opened the solutions and saw five options. I press the old reliable charging attack. '

"First," the gauntlet attachment explained, "shoot the three on the top with the rifle. Then, run up to the two on the bottom by first shooting one with your pistol, and then performing a sweeping leg attack on the other. Finally, pick up the RPG and take out the machine gun turret."

Wow, it did all that just by scanning the environment? "Dul, round up your family, and your men. Get the jeeps ready and we'll get the hell out of here!"

So I followed the steps after the gauntlet told me what to do. "Warning, only four bullets left," I heard it say.

I picked up a used HK416, and started

shooting the ones at the top. They plopped to the ground with a loud thud sound. I dropped the gun and started running towards the two androids, drew my two hidden blades, and leaped on them. When they were eliminated, I quickly scanned the environment with my HEV, and saw where the RPG was. I grabbed it and aimed it at my target with the iron sight. I launched it, and in the next instant all I could see was the huge explosion that left behind only the remains of the turret.

I ran out the godforsaken place, and there were at least twenty-five jeeps coming towards me. From the closest one a hand reached out, and there was Dul saying "Grab hold!"

I caught his hand, and he pulled me into the truck. "My family, and my men will stay in Istanbul while you finish your mission for the Sultan," he said to me. "I hate to tell you this, but I was expecting you these past few days. We'll be with the Sultan until you come back."

I made the jump to the other truck as one of Dul's men unhooked the chain that had been holding them together. It would be a long way to my destination. But my new friend had made it just a little bit shorter.

Chapter XIII
At last

"The greatest discovery of my generation is that man can alter his life simply by altering his attitude of mind."
-James Truslow Adams

It took me a long time to drive across the desert on that truck. I found myself in the middle of nowhere when I arrived. There was nothing there at all. I couldn't believe I failed the mission. The Mosque was nowhere to be found. Everywhere around me was nothing but barren landscape. But then again, the sun was so bright, I couldn't see much other than the reflection off the heated sand. I figured I might as well drive a little bit further and see what there was to see.

As I drove further on, I found something. It looked like a village, maybe even a city. I drove faster, getting closer to it. It was nothing but the ruins of an old city.

"Surya," the gauntlet spoke to me, "you have arrived at your destination. Do you want to quit this navigation?"

I ignored it, staring at the ruins. Empty guns were everywhere and the buildings were broken. The entire city was part of the desert. No roads, no civilization. Nothing.

I was looking around, trying to find the mosque, with no luck. But I did find an old building, destroyed like all the rest. I went in closer to see if it was the building as I had a feeling it was. There was a pathway of brown lines leading to this building as I followed the path in, but then I realized something. The Sultan told me something to remember before entering inside the mosque. Always go in from above, I thought as I remembered his words. This was a tip. So I scanned the environment with my HEV on my hat, and found something so magnificent, the Sultan would never believe it.

There it was shining in the sun, and it was no hallucination. It was real, looking so beautiful. It reminded of Amber. I couldn't resist thinking of her, but then I saw her and Pooja in front of me. It was those damn hallucinations tricking me to make me weaker and weaker. But still I couldn't shake them as I missed my team a lot. I missed Pooja as she would always heal me whenever I was sick. I missed Tommy when he would help me on missions. And most of all, I missed Amber. She was my best friend, and was going to be more, until I went on this stupid mission. I might not even come back alive from this trip. All I could do was try hard, hoping that the Great Indian God of destruction would keep me safe.

I went forward, but as I heard a noise I ran and hid in the sand dunes as I saw the heavy armored robots guarding the entrance to the mosque. I scanned it one more time and saw my second enemy: General Kazem Zahaar. I knew that I had to grab the plans without him noticing me. This meant that I had to be subtle. Subtle enough for them not to notice me. So, I shot my grapnel rope onto the gargoyle on the front of the mosque when the robots were on their patrol route at a different part of the building and got away from the guards to keep them from alerting Zahaar.

Following the Sultan's advice, I went from above where the gargoyles could support my weight. But I had no chance of surviving after looking at the courtyard. It was infested with Notrax troops carrying heavy machine guns everywhere. To avoid them, I had to go in from above. I scanned the environment as I looked for an opening. God, I couldn't find anything even as hard as I was searching.

Luckily, I found an opening in which I could go through. The hallway's roof was open so I could sneak in through. It led to the room where Laroche hid his plans to conquer Istanbul.

As I landed, the hallway was like a living hell. Blood everywhere and rotten corpses that the Notrax had killed. The smell of the rotten flesh was heavy in my nose, distracting me from thinking about my goal, as I thought about the bodies. These must have been the bodies of the Priests and the people that died during the conquest of the Middle East by the Notrax. Images flashed through my head as if I had experienced these things myself.

I shook the images from my mind as I went inside of the room. "Shiva Shiva Shankara, Hara Hara Mahadev," I whispered to myself to calm myself down and to have my guardian god, Shiva, protect me.

The room was large and held a large screen which acted like a monitor. It was connected to a desktop computer with all the files to Laroche's plans, such as the Conquest of the Middle East and the creation of the Notrax army. I searched through the computer folders and kept on scrolling, trying to find anything about the Invasion of Istanbul.

Folder after folder I searched through, until I found one labeled Conquest of the Middle East. As I opened the file, I smiled. Here were the battle plans of the Notrax.

I quickly transferred the information onto my flash-drive the Sultan gave to me. As I was almost finished, I heard a gun being cocked.

"Surya, you try so hard. You will not escape out of here alive," Zahaar said confidently.

"Think again, Zahaar." I turned quickly and shot the General in the leg with my flintlock revolver. I grabbed the flash-drive and escaped out of the room. The robots started shooting as I dodged between every single one of them and a few bullets got closer than was good for comfort. I shot my grapnel rope at the gargoyle and then again was bolting away like a rocket.

A helicopter came down low over the Mosque and I took my chance to escape, clinging on to the side mounted machine gun. As I got inside, I could not believe my luck, or my eyes.

"You're done, Surya, You're done," the Prince of Monaco said as I closed my eyes, finally relaxing. From behind us, I heard the sound of a huge explosion.

They had fired at the Mosque, the base of the evil doers, and destroyed all of the robots. The explosion was immense and there were no survivors. No survivors except one.

"Laroche," Zahaar said, "round up the men."

Chapter XIV
Dragon Valley

"Regard your soldiers as your children, and they will follow you into the deepest valleys; look on them as your own beloved sons, and they will stand by you even unto death."
  -Sun Tzu

After coming back from my mission two days ago, I was in the library of the Grand Palace, reading the diary of Piri Reis. I was recovering from the wounds that I acquired from the mission and had to stay in the hospital until I was well enough to return to my duties.

I read every single thing that was in that diary. From civilizations to weapons to discoveries, it had nothing that would upgrade my team. But I did see something that caught my eye. The page that I wanted to see after hours of reading different books.

It was a page on Dragons, large lizard-like creatures that had different powers as they roamed around the hidden valley of the Taurus Mountains.

The entry on Dragons inside his diary was like this:

"*In my explorations of the many wonders of Turkey, I have found something so magnificent I wanted to record in my diary. Something near the city of Adana lies a village near the Taurus Mountains. Near that village is a cave that leads to a valley. A place full of creatures that are protected for eternity. They are the Dragons that roam around the valley. Villagers complain about the sounds of roaring, but have not discovered any of the beasts themselves. In 1507, Byzantines and the Ottoman Empire soldiers used Leonardo da Vinci's invention, the Gilder, to search from above as they looked for the dragons. Their discovery is detailed here. Although they may reproduce, they must not be harmed at any cost as they're the last of their kind. Only the most powerful ones may be used for battle as they will sacrifice their life for their home and for their children. You shall enter through the portal in the cave after climbing the natural stairs of Ilah, and will find the valley. But I shall tell you as a warning in case you attempt to tame one of the Dragons. The one that will try to kill you will kill you and there is no doubt. If you harm a female Dragon, then she will alert Vadinin sonuncusu."*

After that last sentence, the rest was burnt like someone had tried to destroy it. Vadinin sonuncusu? What the hell was that? Why were the dragons so hard to kill?

I researched the valley on my computer but I could find nothing about it. I didn't find any books about it, and no information about it anywhere, but I did find a photo about the village in a book. It showed normal village life with people trading goods, butchers cutting meat and hanging the carcasses. It was a community with a large marketplace. This was no help, I thought.

But after closing the book, I opened it again and took another look. Sure enough, I saw something peculiar in the background. Something that looked like stairs that led to a cave. I took a map of the place and the picture and took off to the Adana Express, the train that would take me to the village. No one saw me rushing downstairs or getting into the taxi. I told the advisor to the Sultan, "Tell the team I'll be back after I'm done in Adana."

As I was on the train to Adana, it took me across the abandoned villages of Cappadocia, through the plains of Konya, and through the valleys of the Taurus Mountains.

The village near the city of Adana was monumental, with shacks the size of a two story house. Many people were around the market. The marketplace was huge, with three butcher's markets, six trading centers, and four clothing and apparel shops. Although, there was an abandoned shack with no lights. At first, I thought that it was haunted, but as I went forward, I heard a raspy voice, telling me to go in.

I saw a Romani girl, wearing her bandana on her head, a red top with her shoulders showing, and a purple skirt. Her wrist was heavy with braided ropes and bracelets. She remind me a lot of Pooja, with that same youthful beauty.

"Well, aren't you a rather attractive man?" she said, flirting with me. I had never been so disgusted by anyone so fast.

"I didn't come here to flirt," I told her angrily. "I came to seek the valley of the Dragons. Do you know where I could find it?"

"Good man you are Surya, aren't you? Always trying to find something. Come follow me, and you will find the valley. But we must take a horse."

I couldn't believe she knew my name. I only thought that people like the Sultan knew my name, but I didn't know that everyone in this country knew who I was.

I borrowed a horse from the stables with her. As I ascended onto the horse, the gypsy got on the horse behind me, holding me tightly to her. "Now, the trip from here to the valley is very short although going by foot it's dangerous due to the Notrax demons roaming around the plains," she warned seriously.

I took her advice and went with her across the plains of Adana, where the Robots roamed. Robot Smilodons grabbed any predator or prey lurking in the tall grass to escape. Huge creatures with teeth the size of half of a helicopter's wing blade, their speed faster than the speed of a cheetah. But I had no problem with them as I was riding on the horse.

When we got to the entrance of the valley, I

heard the sound of Dragons, roaring in the distance. The valley was hidden behind vines of thick grass hanging down, hiding the entrance from any threat to enter it. The smell of the fire from the Dragon's breath and the sound of their roaring let me know I had arrived.

"Go through here with your horse and you shall enter the portal of the Dragon Valley," the gypsy said.

"Thank you, and Elveda," I responded in Turkish.

"Harika, let's go!" she said as a Dragon appears and she flies away on it. Wow, I just got my first look at a dragon.

The portal was painted a light blue color, still fresh enough after 500 years. It was surrounded by a diamond arch that held the portal together. I was alone now, as my gypsy guide had left. It was probably a good idea if I went through it now as the Notrax troops might catch me. I took my horse through it and everything went black.

I thought it was the end of my life. All I saw was black nothing. It was like that for a few seconds until I saw light.

Light. What could it have been? What was it? I had all these questions as I was curious about the small speck of light. I went closer and closer as my horse shivered, scared. Then, I heard a sound. A sound so fierce, my horse whinnied and panicked at the same time. I calmed her down by patting her on the head and brushing his mane, "Calm down, girl. There, there."

I commanded him to move forward. She went slowly as the light started getting bigger and bigger. I finally reached the end of the light and as my vision started to focus I saw something so magnificent.

Dragons. They were everywhere, flying around, some drinking water by the river that flowed through the valley, some lingering and babies in the nearby caves. A waterfall was adding water to the river. I was all happy and excited that I had found something that no one could have found in a million years. It was so beautiful, just looking at the scenery of the valley, how the dragons flew in the sky, how the rivers shone in the sun, how the mountains stood tall all around. My heart felt warm after looking at this.

But there was another threat. A large dragon landed on the center stone of the valley and breathed fire in the air. It was a large black dragon with horns that looked like the devil. Its wingspan was larger compared to the other dragons. Hold on a second, I thought to myself. I felt like I had read something about a large one greater than any of the other dragons in the valley. Curious, I pulled out Piri's diary and read the second page of the Dragon Valley section where it showed the diagram of the largest dragon. As I looked over the photos, I read how Vadinin sonuncusu is the largest one in the valley and also the protector.

This was the one that I needed to tame. This was mine and I knew in my soul that he would be the one to help us fight. I commanded my horse to jump off the cliff to the ground below.

As I descended off the cliff, the Dragon looked at me fiercely. To be honest, this Dragon was humongous. The size of its head was bigger than my body and its roar was as a loud as thunder booming in the sky. The Dragon flew over to me as the others stood by watching, doing their own thing. I held out my hand, showing it that it could trust me. The Dragon grunted and a heavy gust of wind blew into my face. Again, I held out my hand, slowly waiting for it to come and let me pat its head. As I moved in closer, the Dragon moved in closer too and finally it let me touch it!

It let me pat its head. "Hey Pal. You look like a nice Dragon to me, aren't you? From now on, we will stick together and fight. All right?" I calmly said as I found the beast to be gentle and intelligent. I told the horse to go back to the village. I was going to take my new friend for a test ride. The horse went running away on the natural ramps. Spotting her, another Dragon swooped down and gobbled the horse into its mouth.

I was relaxed as I ascended onto the back of it. All right, think fly, I told myself. "Fly towards those mountains, friend," I said, and the Dragon went dashing straight for the mountains. After flying so fast, I felt nauseous. I was scared for a moment when we were about to crash into the mountain. Scared to death, I shut my eyes tightly and waited for the pain of the impact. I opened my eyes when I realized that I didn't crash into a mountain. I was in the air. The Dragon had saved me, taking me in the air.

I could see everything in the sky, from the troops guarding every section of the plains to the people following their normal lifestyle. I could smell the Butcher's market from up top and hear the animals making sounds. Usually whenever I learn to ride something new on my own, I have trouble with it, but now I knew I was born to be a Dragon Rider. I had that skill to tame any Dragon in the valley. But, I needed to get home as fast as I could. It was six o'clock in the afternoon already and I needed to come back to the Palace to show the Sultan what I had acquired.

Chapter XV
Rescue

"I went to Fort Bragg and learned that Delta was indeed gearing up for the rescue. Still I was concerned the Reagan staff would not be willing to take the risk of sending an official military force into Laos."
    -Bo Gritz

After bonding with my dragon, I decided to name him. He was the last of his kind yet the most powerful of all of the dragons. So since he was the leader of the dragons and the most powerful, I decided to name him Pendragon, after Urther Pendragon.

It was an afternoon of a Friday that I came back from the valley in the Taurus Mountains near Adana on Pendragon's back. It took me about two hours to come back to Istanbul, but as soon as I came back, I saw there was another problem. This time, the damage was massive. This time, something worse had happened.

I went running inside the Palace, after I dismounted off Pendragon and slammed the doors of the Palace open. The destruction of the Palace's interior was worse than the city. It had a hole in the dome, the Sultan's throne and Princess Kyla's throne were destroyed, broken into pieces. The shelves were on fire, the books burning, and many people were on the ground, dead. Body parts were scattered everywhere around the hall.

I found Kyla on the ground, weeping. "Hey, what happened?" I asked her.

"He came, Surya! He came. He took my father and Amber."

Anger overcame me. All of a sudden, I had that feeling that I wanted to rip out his heart. Laroche! No one harms my friends or family and if they do, they won't live to see the next day. Snarling, I ran out of the Palace. Pendragon was waiting outside.

"Pendragon, I just got you as my pet. But we're going to have to do something insane, and you're not going to like it." I warned him as I ascended his back. I put a bracelet on his huge wrist that would allow him to come to me when I called. Pendragon breathed fire in the air as a signal for take off and he launched himself into the sky.

As we rode across the Taurus Mountains and we came near the asylum of Mount Ararat, I saw some of Laroche's men, guarding the entrance into the asylum.

"Pendragon, buddy. I need you to create a distraction for them right there. I'll press a button on my gauntlet to let you know when I need you. Just drop me off at the roof, ok?" I asked him. He responded back with a snarl. I couldn't tell whether or not it was a yes or a no, but I believed it was a yes.

He dashed across the plains as fast as possible. I was worried about Amber, and I wondered if she was okay.

Pendragon dropped me off on the roof, and he landed in front of the troops. Both of them started shooting at Pendragon with AK-47 rifles and he snarled in pain. Hurt, he fled away from the troops with minimal injuries.

"That's right, you damn dirty dragon! You fly away and never come back, otherwise we cook you and serve it to the captain!" one of them yells.

"Tommy, are you there?" I called to him

through the communication link in my gauntlet.

He answered almost at once. "Surya, Kyla told me your location and now I just sent you the overview map of the asylum. It shows the location of the Sultan and Amber. By the way, what the hell happened? Why did Laroche come back?"

"He knows I'm here. And he's angry. So he kidnapped Amber and the Sultan knowing I would come for them," I respond weakly as I viewed the map of the asylum, finding them on the map.

I figured if I could find Laroche, then I could find them. I landed on the glass softly, careful not to break it. I looked through the glass and saw that the troops were armed with AK-47 and M4 carbine rifles. Laroche must have told them to shoot anything that came in his way, because there were an awful lot of those heavy armored troops waiting by the door, carrying machine guns.

To avoid any attention from the guards, I slowly stepped on the glass, checking to see if a part of it was able to carry me across the building. I opened up my HEV on my hat to see if that was the right room where he held both Amber and the Sultan. As I found the room, I took out a device that would connect to my hat and would help me hear conversations through thick walls or from a distance.

"You have betrayed me, Sultan," Laroche was saying. "You said you wouldn't call him. I told you if you did that I would terminate you. I would have given you one more chance, but sadly I cannot. I have beaten you till you are almost dead, there is no chance for Surya to come and save you at this moment," he threatened as I heard him beating the Sultan up.

Gasping and coughing between words, the Sultan spoke up, "You're...wrong, Laroche. He will...come and kill you. He...will not accept death... unless he has saved his loved ones. Even though I may die today, he...will...avenge...my death. He...will...kill...you!"

Shocked by the statement, Laroche lifted a gun. "You have just proven worthless," I heard Laroche say, and then he shot the Sultan in the head. I viewed his status on HEV and it said deceased. If only I had come earlier, then I could have saved him and Amber.

"Now that I am done with him, I shall do

whatever I want with you." He was touching Amber in a way that didn't just make me angry, but infuriated me. Boiling with anger, the gauntlet knew my feeling, and enabled the maximum strength, and I crashed through the roof, landing on and injuring Laroche.

I felt more power as I threw him across the room. Because of his strength, the wall was damaged, breaking around him, and he couldn't get up.

I took out my shotgun and shot him in the chest. It didn't do any real damage but it disabled his entire body, which gave us a good amount of time to escape. I held her by the waist and shot my grapnel at the roof, pulling us both up.

As Amber and I were on the roof, Pendragon was next to the building, waiting for me as I summoned him to come and rescue us. We mounted quickly, and I urged the great Dragon up. As we took off, the Notrax troops came out and started shooting with their guns.

Unfortunately, I got shot by a pistol. In pain, I couldn't hold on any longer to Pendragon's saddle as I lost my grip. I fell to the ground, unconscious from falling off Pendragon.

Laroche woke up some time after Surya shot him in the chest, disabling his body. He was furious that Surya had escaped with Amber, but had some pleasure in the fact that one of his troops had shot Surya.

"Captain, are you okay?" one of his troops asked as he threw a temper tantrum, breaking the tables in half and making dents in the wall.

The troops could hear his muffled voice through the door. "Declare war on the Turkish. We will take the country no matter what happens. Next week is the war and we will fight till we get what belongs to us!"

Then he shot the body of the Sultan with his pistol again, and again, until his anger was gone. "Damn humans."

Chapter XVI
The Cave

"Love isn't something you find. Love is something that finds you."

-Loretta Young

After I fell off the dragon, I couldn't feel anything in my body. Blood was pouring out of my shoulder. After I found shelter, I was no better off, laying there, wondering about Amber.

It was dark and cold and I couldn't sleep. With the pain in my arm and worrying about Amber, wondering where she was, I couldn't sleep at all. As I lay there awake, I saw something. Something that made a fiery breath. It created a ring of fire that shined brightly in the dark sky. Then I realized what it was. It was a beast. A beast that had wings with a long snout and horns that resembled the same as my dragon.

As I got out of my cave, I saw the beast land and a girl dismount from it. I saw her and recognized her immediately, knowing that she had come for me. I ran to her, but fell, finding myself still bleeding from the infected bullet that was still lodged in my shoulder. I couldn't walk on my feet.

Amber came running over to help me get on my feet. She isn't disgusted by my bleeding or the infection. "Put your arm around me," she said, "and I will help you. I promise."

"I don't know. The infection is pretty bad."

"Trust me."

So I did, but I felt really bad about putting so much on her. Although it was okay for her, it was never okay for me. I was supposed to be her protector. Not the other way around.

She took me back to the cave where I rested for the night. Pendragon was in a tree, sleeping after a bad day for him and me. Yet, I still I don't know why Pendragon was feeling injured. I mean, I'm the one with all the injuries.

Amber pulled out something from her satchel. A small container filled with a kind of lotion. She removed my jacket and my shirt, and checked out the injury. "Oh my! This is...well...too much.   But I have the correct cure. Eucalyptus based lotion. It will be cured in no time. Well, approximately six hours."

As she rubbed the lotion on my arm, I couldn't stop thinking about her. How her eyes glistened more than the stars and how her hair blew with the wind kept my mind off my injury. "I know what I said back at the asylum. You didn't hear any of it, right?"

"I heard all of it," I said. "I'm guessing it was all true."

She leaned over and kissed me on the lips. It was amazing! I couldn't believe it. This just made my night.

She smiled at me with one of those smiles that she did so well. "Would I have kissed you if it wasn't true? Surya. You are my boyfriend, and I couldn't ask for a better one than you. I love you with all my heart and I never want to leave you."

What have you done, Surya? I thought. I couldn't believe it. Throughout the years, she always loved me as a friend. She liked me even though I was a geek. But, I never knew she loved me in this way. Maybe that was the reason why she dumped Peter. I mean, this was the beginning of a beautiful relationship. I was shocked to have her kiss me. Especially her, the President's daughter. But it was time I confessed something to her.

"Amber, I have a confession to make. People think of me as a person who always has his mind on protecting the world from danger. A person who trains throughout his life. But every night, I think about you in my dreams, hoping that you are protected and safe. Because in my heart, half of it belongs to my family, but the other half belongs to you."

Shocked that I had the same feelings for her, Amber realized that I was perfect for her, and that she would never leave me

We sleep inside the cave for the night as Pendragon went to sleep with us next to the cave. She wrapped herself around me while we slept, and I got that feeling in my heart.

I found love, I found love, I thought.

Chapter XVII
Finch

"I am sometimes a fox and sometimes a lion. The whole secret of government lies in knowing when to be the one or the other."

-Napoleon Bonaparte

In the morning, Amber and I returned on Pendragon's back. Tommy designed a leash that would help me understand what he was trying to tell me. But, my next goal was to find the man that matched the long strand of black hair that had fought against the Notrax on the morning of the invasion. It took about two weeks to track him down. To find out his location in the country. After two weeks of research to track this man down, I finally found him. He was in the slums of Ankara. I printed his photo, and flew off with Pendragon.

The slums were a cold and harsh place, filled with things that are really scary in a way that so many people couldn't even imagine. The roads were broken. People were using rags as clothes. The only place that didn't look so poor was a bar. A bar that had lights on in it, and looked like there was a party going inside there.

So I went inside. If I was going to find the man anywhere, it would most likely be here.

My phone started ringing as I entered the place. I saw who was calling and answered the phone. "Surya, it's Tommy. I found his location and he's not a merchant at all. He works there. He's coming to where you are. I just tracked him. I think you should see him by now."

I didn't see anyone. So I sat down at a random table with a guy wearing a dirty white shirt that looked like it came from the dumpster. The waiter dropped the cup on the table. "Here's your drink. Enjoy."

The cup plopped on the ground, and almost half the rum spilled out. I tried to drink what rum was left, but it smelled so bad, like it came from a cow's behind. It looked muddy as it made a sloshing sound.

"I know how you feel," a man said next to me. "The ambience here sucks, and so do their beverages. All just a piece of crap."

The guy seemed reasonable, and he agreed with my feelings about this godforsaken place. "Get out of my seat before I kick your sorry butt," he said.

I turned around and saw a guy who was really infuriated with me.

"Why should I get up when I'm already sitting down?" I said as a response. He took out a revolver, and pointed it at my head. The other man talking to me stands up and pointed a sawed off shotgun at his head. He cocks the gun, yet the big and bulky guy smacked the guy with his shotgun. It shot into the air and it clattered to the ground.

"Nobody move," he said. "If you are willing to pay the money to live, you just simply drop it on the ground and get out. Those that don't have no money, get out and never come back! Get out!"

Everybody started running away, except the three belly dancers. The red, the blue and the purple clad dancers yell at him that they weren't afraid of his shotgun or him.

He pointed the shotgun at them. "You

wouldn't hurt girls, no?" the girls start whimpering.

"Watch me."

They all started running away, and I started walking away, too. "No," he said to me, "you stay."

I stayed, fearful that he might do something to me. "I know who you are, and I know you are looking for me. My name is Darius Finch, and I think Byziwad sent you here, no? But you should know that I am also an enemy of the Notrax General Zahaar. I see you want me to join, and to fight with you to help save Istanbul, but as you can see, I am not qualified to be on your side. I can release something so powerful that cannot turn it off afterwards.

"You're a mutant," I realized. "My team is full of mutants. Pooja, my sister, has the powers of the gods. Tommy, my best friend, has inhuman brains but also the strength. And Amber, my girlfriend, has the sight of an eagle. But we're not complete yet. To complete our team, you must join us. If you want to get rid of that tyrant, join me and we will destroy him."

Darius accepted my request to join his team and to kill Zahaar once and for all. He was going to be on my team for as long as we stayed together. "Darius, welcome to our team."

Chapter XVIII
Unleashing the Beast

"He who is unable to live in society, or who has no need because he is sufficient for himself, must be either a beast or a god."

    -Aristole

"We will start the final war next week. We will destroy the Grand Palace, so they could mourn over the loss of their precious Sultan and the symbol of Istanbul," Laroche's voice drones on as Tommy, Pooja, and I hear the recording. It was the next day after I had recruited Finch. I was recovering still from the painful injury on my shoulder. Only a week left before the war starts. As far as I knew, I have recruited some of the greatest warriors in Turkey. From Dragons, to gunners, to archers, and to cavalry, my army is as invincible as they could ever be.

"So here is where the archers stay," I pointed out. "Our army will be charging towards Notrax in the city. The gunners will ride horses, leading the cavalry in the forest."

"As far as I know, the civilians are not aware of this situation. We should evacuate them somewhere else, but where?" Dul asks me.

"Evacuate them to Cappadocia," I directed. "There are empty homes there. Make sure all the Dragons have bonded with the riders. They will take the air, while Finch takes the lead of the ground. He will transform into the Black Lion while you lead horses and cavalry. You are taking the ground with Tommy. Finch will be taking the city while Pooja surrounds the Grand Palace with a force field. Amber and I will take the air along with the rest of the air troops. Distribute the plans among the entire army and we should be good."

A few hours later, Darius and I were at the training ground near Topkapi Palace. The Training ground was huge as each section measured about fifteen acres. The entire training ground was unnaturally silent. "Darius, the reason I brought you here is that you are one of the strongest members of the team. I found you because of this," I held out the long strand of the Black Lion's mane.

Darius was confused for a second. He had a puzzled look on his face. I could tell that he was lying. "Fine, but this is making my life miserable, Surya. I can't turn back to Darius after the Black Lion has been unleashed. That's why I call him 'The Mindless Beast' and other names," he responded in a worried tone.

"But you will turn back to Darius and with my help, the Black Lion will be able to have a mind," I say confidently. I knew my plan was going to work. I gave him a gauntlet with only one button on it. "This gauntlet, created by Tommy, can tell when Darius wants to be let out. You might call it your wake up call."

Darius chuckles. "Surya, if I were you, then I would back off."

He closed his eyes and took deep breaths as he relaxed his mind. It took him a few seconds to relax. As soon he was done, he opened his eyes and he had the eyes of a Lion. He fell to the ground on his knees, moaning. Black hair was growing fast out of his skin as his mouth became the mouth of a predator. His shirt was ripping as his back grew bigger and his hands turned into paws with really sharp nails. As he stood up, he was taller. His pants were ripped and had fallen off. That's when I knew there was hope for Istanbul.

He had turned into the most horrific creature ever: a Black Lion standing on its hind legs. As it punched the ground, it cracked and his steps shook the ground. The beast was infuriated, roaring at me and trying to kill me as I dodged its attacks. One after the other, this thing kept trying to kill me as I tried to injure it with my Urumi. It grabbed onto my Urumi with its mouth, and threw it off to the side where I couldn't reach it. That's when I knew I was screwed.

I turned on the HEV immediately to check my surroundings for any weapons that would give me time to turn the Black Lion back into Darius.

Scanning, I found a metal hammer, a sledgehammer, but it was good enough to injure it or at least land an attack once. So as I ran from my cover, the Black Lion grabbed my shirt and threw me across the training ground, cracking the wall and my back. I was feeling stunned for a while, but I realized that I was ten feet away from the sledgehammer, and the Black Lion wasn't out of breath, but eager to kill me. I quickly enabled Magnetic Mode and pointed my hand to it. The Sledgehammer quickly went flying into my hand and in the nick of time, I dodged the attack of the Black Lion and swung my hammer across the face of the beast. I tried to injure him in the leg, to give me a chance to knock him unconscious.

After wounding the Black Lion, I initiated the change to turn it back into Darius. I felt bad about the amount of damage caused by the Sledgehammer. Soon the transformation commenced and he was back to an average sized human. He was naked, so I gave him my towel to help protect him from humiliation.

"You see, Darius? That monster inside of your body knows that you want to be let out. That device you have on your shoulder will stay on there forever to control it. This is an example of what we will do to the Notrax. But for now, rest. Tomorrow, the war commences."

He nodded in satisfaction, knowing that there is hope for Istanbul. And I thought the same.

Chapter XIX
The Battle for Istanbul

"Whenever death may surprise us, let it be welcome if our battle cry has reached even one receptive ear and another hand reaches out to take up in our arms."
-Che Guevara

"All right, Enable all mechanical horses, I repeat enable all mechanical horses. Switch to war mode and turn on built-in turrets. All ground troops are enabled. Cannons ready, patrols and soldiers ready. Snipers are placed on top and the remaining are with Laroche." informs Notrax Command Center. "All aircraft, loaded. Cargo ship ready. Gunships, now's the time to lift off."

The troops were getting ready to conquer and claim the land after the battle. The aircraft left as the robots cheered, "Yeah, that's right! Show em' who's boss!"

Heavy Armored robots docked inside the Cargo Airplane as the ship started to take off.

All of the Sniper robots equipped with

Biotech Snipers and had been repaired with full body armor to be placed on top of the buildings on the Notrax side of the battlefield. The Robots covered each part of Turkey. The Ground Troops took the forest haven of Istanbul. The aircraft took the sky, and the cannons, turrets and the Sniper troops took the central Istanbul.

As the cargo ship descended near the forest floor, the Golems hopped off the plane while the regular troops jumped off the ship. The Robot Golems got dropped off by the forest floor along with the troops.

"All right boys. Time to conquer this country now. I want to see my new wife in the morning, and I want to plant my posterior on that throne tomorrow morning," Laroche commanded all of the troops in the air and on the ground. "Remember, they're out there folks, stalking you."

The Dragons soared in the air with riders on top of them. Amber flew with me on Pendragon. He screeched and the other dragons respond back. "Guys," I said, "time to rock and roll."

All the dragons attached themselves against

the wall. "Hucum!" Dul cried out as Pendragon screeched to command all of the dragons to attack the fleet of Gunships in the air.

"All forces, select your automated machine guns and start firing." the driver of the leader gunship ordered. Pendragon leapt onto the leading gunship while all the other dragons imitated him. I witnessed a dragon eat a Notrax trooper's head off. Most off the dragons started by destroying the gunships, but some of them get shot and suffered injury.

"Hold on," the commanding trooper says. "Goddamnit! Patrols, hold your fire and view your radars. General, assemble all troops to their correct positions, and find cover. All Robo-Scramblers, transform into physical form and find out what going's on from the other side."

The leader hears the booming sounds of the enemy fleet coming their way as their radar showed the enemy as red. It pounded to a rhythmic pattern. To the general, it sounded like horses running, but then he heard the battle cry of the Turkish horse riders, "En binmek edelim!"

All of the other riders repeat the leader's

words as the Black Lion roars and shreds the Robo-Scramblers to pieces.

"What the hell? Oh my god, shoot them, would ya?!"

All the riders started shooting their rifles as the heavy armored guards started charging towards the army, only to die after the Black Lion leaped off a tree and stands up on its hind legs. "Stinkin' robots" he snarled in disgust as he tears into the metal forms.

The Dragons were on the side of the buildings, trying to stalk the robots as they manned their gunships to the Hagia Sophia.

"All robots, prepare your missiles. Commencing Citadel attack in three, two, on--"

Pendragon roared as the head of the Notrax Aircraft team stopped the countdown. All the other Dragons were signaled and attacked the gunships, grasping their feet onto the blades of the gunship and tearing them apart.

"All right, Tommy, I need you to signal the Black Lion to attack near the forest troops, you understand?"

"Surya! Surya! We're getting creamed. Laroche's ground troops are coming in strong and retreat is imminent!"

I was furious when I heard that. "Don't say retreat! Never fall back! I'll assign some of my men to attack the forest. Dul, take your men and attack at the forest," I ordered Dul and told Tommy to watch for him.

"That's the one, get it!" Laroche ordered his troops to kill Surya and Pendragon. The missiles were being launched even he was dodging them. They sailed past and hit the buildings.

"Alpha three, I want you to call two other gunships and try to kill that guy on the big dragon. Sibilus Protocol seven, I want to you to commence the destruction. Rest of you, engage all hostiles."

All the Dragons were being shot as the enemy found their weak spots. Many people were dying and that's what Laroche wanted to see. The Turkish army couldn't fight back as the Notrax had too much power. It seemed hopeless.

Amber's life flashed before her eyes as the missiles attempted to attack the Dragon. She squeezed me tightly, not letting go if me. "Amber, it's okay. I'm here with you."

As I calmed her down, her hands loosened around my abdomen. "All right, Pendragon, I want you to go to the city and breathe your fire to take out those cannons."

He snarled, taking me to the city as fast as he could. His wings were folded back, bolting like lightning.

I saw the city in a horrible state. The people were dying from the sniper soldiers and cannons. The buildings were burning and there were flames everywhere caused by the flamethrower troops. Soon, the entire battlefield would be wiped clean of the Turkish army. Notrax heavy armored troops were roaming around the street as the Black Lion climbed on top of a building, surrendering himself, knowing there was nothing more he could do. I pressed the button that transformed him back into his human form. "You did well soldier, you did well," I compliment Darius quietly as he was tired and couldn't fight the robots anymore.

"All soldiers, retreat. I'll handle this now." I command my factions. The words were as ashes in my mouth.

I didn't want to draw any attention by having Pendragon throw a fireball, but as I landed safely on the ground, the cannons found me anyway and shot cannonballs that crashed into the spot where I landed with Amber.

Chapter XX
Final

"In the final choice a soldier's pack is not so heavy as a prisoner's chains."
-Dwight D. Eisenhower

I couldn't tell whether or not any of my army was still alive. I couldn't see anything beyond the heavy dust in the air. I stood up coughing and clenching onto my sword. The rest of the crew evacuated to the deserted area of Cappadocia, except one person.

Amber was still there with me. I didn't know what to do. I couldn't find any more transportation to take her back to Cappadocia.

As the sand started to clear up, I finally discovered where I was. I was in the middle of the battlefield, with the enemy army there, waiting for me. I saw Amber running to me to see if I was okay. As she reached me, she stroked my hair, crying at all of my injuries. Her tears started to land on my face. I got up on my feet, and faced the army. I saw Laroche sitting on a rock, Zahaar on a mechanical horse, and the army in place with snipers on both sides of them.

"Surya, this kingdom is now mine, and your place to live is in hell!" Laroche speaks up.

"Hold on, Laroche," Zahaar said, at his ease. "Surya! I've made my friend here a promise to hand over the kingdom to him. Be a good man, and hand over the kingdom to Laroche. If you do, I'll spare your life."

I speak up, gathering my courage, and answered him. "I made a promise too, Zahaar. Hand the traitor over, and I'll spare your army, and you."

"Ha, you'll spare me? I'm nothing less than god! If you are a true man and have the power to kill my entire army, I'll send a hundred robots in their place, and they will kill you and the girl! If you have the power to survive that, I'll leave the kingdom alone!"

"You can send as many robots as you want, Zahaar!" I respond back. "I'll take every one of them! And then I'll come for you!"

"You will suffer once you look at them!"

"I don't care if there are one, or a hundred and one robots! Make sure there is not one less robot."

"If one robot survives you lose."

I thought this was a fair challenge, but I wanted to make it more challenging for me. "Don't send them in one by one, Zahaar. Send them all at once."

"All this talking will not show your power, Surya. Actions always speak louder. Send in the demon robot army!" he ordered.

As the verbal confrontation between Zahaar and me finished, booming footsteps came to my ears, and I saw his army rushing towards me.

I pressed the button to summon Pendragon.

"Amber, I won't spare him," I say to her. "I will cut off his head and make sure his metal head rolls across the battlefield as you watch his blood bathe the ground as a tribute to Allah."

I turned around and knelt on one knee. Raising my sword to the heavens I gripped the sword's blade firmly, drawing it down my skin, so that the first blood that was on my sword is my own.

I wiped the blood on my hand, and smear it on my forehead. I settle my hat, and get ready for whatever would come next. "Start," I call to Zahaar with a smile.

I charged towards the army as they ran towards me, and I dove between their knees, while the robots huddled in between. I jumped in the middle, and stuck out at a robot's face. Zahaar grins and counts. I took out robot after robot, keeping my own count as I went.

"Thirteen robots," Zahaar sneered. "Regular warriors can take out more than that."

I took a spear and shoved it through the nearest robot's heart, then grabbed his sword and cut the next one's head off. As the next one was coming at me, I simply struck it across its chest. Hydrogen starts pouring out as the next one slips and falls into flames. The endoskeleton of the robot was burning and showing as the flame became bigger and bigger.

"Hey Twenty three, you stupid robots, attack from behind!" Zahaar ordered.

I kept on fighting and never fell once while fighting against the robots. I cut one's head off and once the robot's head came off, the view of the Hindu locket on my neck reflected the blood of the robot.

As I kept on fighting, Dark Archer, the archer assassin, aimed for my chest with her crossbow. As she used her aimbot, she shot me in the chest.

I backed up and immediately, stumbling, falling to the ground as she shoots another arrow. My face falls on the sandy ground as the blood starts flowing out of my body.

Amber starts crying as she sees me dying in front of her. The robots want to use their swords to finish me off, but as Amber started running to me, they saw her and charged at her. "Surya!" she yelled.

I heard her voice, and my eyes immediately opened up. I saw her standing there with the robots coming at her with their swords. I had to act. I shot a spear across the field. The spear killed all of the robots and they slid across the field coming to rest at the feet of the President's daughter.

I stood up all bloody and weak, but I

grabbed another spear on the ground and killed the Dark Archer with it.

"Eighty four," I counted for Zahaar. I was losing my energy reserves as I fought my way through the sixteen robots remaining. As I did, Zahaar started to shed tears in actual sympathy for me.

There were three more robots left. I was limping, I was weak, and I was bleeding as I killed them one after the other. I ran to the robots, jumped on their heads, killed the first two, and as the last robot fell to the ground, I dug the sword into its chest.

As I killed the last one, blood started to come out of my mouth. Zahaar ripped the Notrax flag off its pole and threw it into to the flames, his feeling swayed as I had fought against ninety-nine of his best men, not only to save the country, but to protect everyone from the evil the Notrax represent.

"Enough, Zahaar? Do you want to send more in?"

Instead of ordering his troops to kill me, he does something else. "Wonderful!" he shouts. He comes running to me and puts one hand on my shoulder, shedding tears. He says with amazement, "Surya, I've seen kings give up their own cities for me to conquer from nothing more than a glance from me. Armies surrender at the sound of my name. Though your heart is bleeding, you still killed your enemies. You were willing to sacrifice your life to save the entire city,"

He yelled and knelt on one leg, and said to me very seriously, "I, General Kazem Zahaar, am now a servant of yours due to your bravery."

As he hands his axe to me, Laroche came in and kicked me in the face, making blood run down my face.

"Laroche, why would you kick him?" Zahaar asked in surprise, standing up to protect me.

"You gave your word, Zahaar! You said you would help me kill him and take over Istanbul! Now, where's that promise you've made? Are you finally breaking it?"

He knew as a general, he could not break any promise he made to a fellow captain. "Forgive me, Surya!" He furiously bent his axe and threw it on the ground, hating himself for the position he had put himself in. He shed his tears at the sight of me suffering from my wounds. But I was ready. Ready to fight again.

Chapter XXI
Death of a Creation

"I have never killed a man, but I have read many obituaries with great pleasure."
   -Clarence

I was on the sandy ground, beaten up, cut, bruised, stabbed, and shot. But, I knew that I wouldn't stop fighting until Laroche's blood splattered all over the sword of Allah. I got up while Amber stayed on the ground, crying about how I was trying to risk my life for everyone I love.

Laroche winked at Amber as he used his magnetic hands to pick up selected weapons. He picked up two swords. I had my Urumi and my sword in my hand. He threw a sword at my shoulder, but I blocked it with my sword. He picked up another one and struck me on the back, which I dodged enough so that all I got was a painful mark.

I fell back while Amber came in and helped me get up. Her hand was covered with my blood.

"Hey Amber," Laroche said with a smile, "put him back in the battle or you'll die with him."

Amber still didn't let go of me. I got up to protect her. Laroche tried to strike me with his sword but missed. I threw my sword at him. His prosthetic skin got damaged from the blow. He stroked it to see how bad it was. Not that bad, but it made him angry.

He charged towards me and I did the same. He jumped, taking out his dagger to stab me in the heart, but it was too late because I stabbed him in the heart before he could.

He turned and said to Amber, "If I die, then you'll die with me."

He threw the dagger at Amber, but missed her. I felt pure anger boiling inside of me. My eyes turned red and the desire to kill him once and for all overwhelmed me. I dig the dagger deep inside his heart, and then I took my sword, and rip his head off for the final move.

Suddenly, there was dead silence. The peaceful moment was followed by the Notrax sniper robots evacuating the entire city. Now that the robot Laroche had died, they ran away.

Amber ran to me, taking my head gently in her hands, "Surya! Surya!"

"Amber, I made a promise to god that I will not accept death until I have saved my friends and this country. Now that time has come. I shall seal my sleep with a final look of your face."

I saw Tommy and Pooja, coming towards me. Then everything went dark.

Epilogue

Surya did not die. He was being healed of the severe injuries in his body. Shot and stabbed, cut and bruised, he was weak. Weak enough that he couldn't talk, only scream from the pain.

Laroche was dead after the battle, and the pain in Surya's heart was eased when he finally ripped off Laroche's head. Surya's battle against the robots was telecasted all over the internet and other video sharing websites. "I saw his face, and I immediately felt different about him," one of the citizens said, reflecting on how he had saved her life. People sold Prince of India merchandise. Fake fedoras, toy gauntlets, a plush model of his dragon, even Barbie dolls of his entire team. The world knew his name and he became a figure of justice.

But as soon as he recovered from his injuries, there was a day where he had to meet his punishment at the Royal Court of Justice.

I had attracted the attention of the world, as people built shrines, Indians treated me as their saviour, and most of all, people everywhere were thanking me. I was getting texts and messages from all over the world. Letters from families whose relatives lost their life to the tyrant, Laroche.

But, this was the end of the happiness for me. Two days after the battle, just recovered from my wounds, I got a court summons from the Royal Court of Justice in Sofia, Bulgaria. I hoped this was not some kind of punishment for me.

But I knew better.

So I traveled there and I met with the royal council made up of a leader of each country. They appeared as holograms and spoke to other council members and to me.

"Surya, the first thing you built was a robot. A robot meant to fight with you in wars. To work with the royal council in order to help us deal with war. But war became even more powerful and deadly after this robot became a terrorist. Killing innocent people. We thought to punish you for this and we..."

The Chief of Tanzania, the leader of the Royal Council, stopped as I interrupted him. He stopped talking as I spoke my mind to say something important. "Before this was a world where war such as we just fought became a waking nightmare, I was protecting my country, not only because god made me like this, but to show the enemy that humans are unstoppable. And we showed them. If you want to lay consequences on me for what I have created, I understand. But the world won't last long without my help," I made a point that I hoped the Chief would understand.

The council took a long time to respond to me. The President of the United States spoke up, "Chief, before you start talking, I have decided one thing: let this boy go back to the world. His consequences have already been great. Well, guess what? I don't care. And I am talking to the entire council when I say that this boy will stay with his family and protect our world so we will have a prosperous future. Say aye if you agree with me."

The President made his point as the council said aye, due to my bravery in the last battle, and the generous words of the President of the United States.

I made a promise that I would protect our world for the people. Later after my team packed up their bags to head back to their home country, Kyla wanted to see us downstairs.

"Surya, if my father was here, he would have thanked you sincerely for saving his mother country. But as a token of appreciation, I wanted to do this." She kissed me on the cheek. I was feeling a bit down knowing I was going to leave Kyla forever, so I made a decision.

"Kyla, I liked you as a friend, but I realized I may never see you again in the future. So I want to give you this."

It was a portable hologram caller, something I could use to always stay in touch. As she was crying tears of joy, she hugged me as tight as possible and left the room, crying.

I held Amber's hand tightly as we left, thinking this was the start of a beautiful beginning. So as Tommy, Pooja, Amber and I rode through the city, taking one final look, I hugged both Pooja and Amber, as Tommy and I fist-bumped each other and we all said one final word as we set off into the sunset.

"Friends forever together."

Two years later, Laroche's eyes started to

power up as his fingers twitch.   He had one last thought in his mind before shutting down again.

I'll be back, Surya.

Dragon Valley Setting Concept Art

Take a sneak peek at the next book

Prince of India
The Mark of the Assassin

Prologue

The KGC, the Knights of the Golden Circle, were a group in the Confederate States, planning to kill one of our presidents that changed the entire United States. "Mark my words, David Smith. You will forever be sorry to leave our group. We will be known forever as the greatest society history will record," said John Wilkes Booth

I refused to kill our sixteenth president Abraham Lincoln, not only because he fought for the slaves and changed the United States, but he was my ally in the war and a close friend of mine.

It was morning, where everything was all peaceful and quiet. The neighbors started working on their crops for the harvesting season. I went to the White House to see how everything was going. Mary Todd was in her lounge, relaxing as usual, the cook and the staff running all over the place with the morning's duty. As I entered the oval office, I was confronted by two guards. "Check him to see if he's safe."

"Gentlemen, let him pass through." The guards left the room as President Lincoln stood up.

The tall man with the beard took off his glasses and put on his suitcoat. He was in the middle of signing some important document.

"Good mornin' Mister. Lincoln, I needed to tell you something. You see, I was a spy for the KGC. I warn you to stay here in the White House. You're darn safe here. They said they were going to kill you."

"Pish posh, young man. Look, you are my greatest ally, and my best friend. I understand why you were at the KGC base. But to kill me? No, no, no. This is plain nonsense. I think you need a nice, steaming bowl of soup made by our best chefs in the White House. Chef Mclaughlin, bring this young man a bowl of your finest vegetable tomato soup."

President Lincoln wasn't believing a word I said. I tried to tell him about the assassination, but still he thought that the war was over. Then he invited me to Ford's theater to see the play, "Our American Cousin."

So the night came on. I decided to take my weapons to the theater. I wore my gauntlet, full of gadgets such as a hidden blade, dagger launcher, and smoke bomb launcher. I took my flintlock pistol and put my bow and my quiver around my back. My grappling hook got tucked in the belt of my suit. I called my horse, Bhairav over, and rode over to Ford's theater.

Ford's theater was once a house of worship, where people would come to pray each Sunday. Then it became this theater where Mister Lincoln wanted me to watch the play "Our American Cousins." For me it was kind of boring. But I guess since the President wanted to see the play, I would have to watch it. I am a poor man with no money so I would be forced to steal and sneak in. As a master assassin, I was very qualified for it. I would sneak in through a loose tile in the roof, and I then climb over to the seats in the theater.

I knew there was something fishy was going on. I went in for proper investigation.

As soon as we reached the second portion of the play, I saw someone coming up behind President Lincoln. It wasn't the general. He was standing near Mary Todd. He pointed a gun to the President's head.

I yelled, "Mister Lincoln, look out!" But it

was too late. The assassin fired his weapon, and Mister Lincoln fell to the floor, holding his head. The man who shot Lincoln fell off the stage, and the US flag got caught on his boot.

As soon as he landed, I knew it was John Wilkes Booth, one of the members of the KGC. He took out a dagger and yelled out, "Sic Semper Tyrannus!"

I tried shooting him, but I missed the shot with my bow and arrow. He wobbled over to the backstage, and out the building, and got on his horse. I almost shot his horse, but I missed again. He ran off somewhere to hide.

Mister Lincoln! I ran as fast as I could to see him. I climbed up the wall and saw the stream of blood running down the wall. As I got to the seats, he wasn't there. But then, there was something so suspicious. Booth wasn't planning to kill him at first, but to kidnap him. I cried the entire time, and was mourning the loss of my beloved friend. I knew that the war hadn't ended.

It had only begun.

Acknowledgements

I would like to thank my best friends Connor Mehlenbacher and Jackson Coyne for supporting me in writing this book. I would also like to thank a few people for being part of the Prince of India team. First, I would like to thank Elicia Mcguinness, Jodie Dukes, Pamela Ankrum, Amanda Easter, Jennifer Shubert Finch, Adam Finch, Shawn Wells and Jennifer Trosclair for helping me edit my book. They all helped me express something I truly enjoy. For helping me with the drawings, I would like to thank Ivan Cirovic in Uzice, Serbia, a good friend of mine and an excellent artist. For creating the magnificent cover, I would like to thank Roland Ali Suello Pantin. For creating the music, voices and main presentation for my book distribution, I would like to thank Lewis Andrew for his outstanding work. I also would like to thank my family and my little sister, Aishu, who supported me and told me that I could write this book. In closing, I would like to thank a few friends of mine: Hailey MacNealy, Matthew Carter, Nathan Fisher, Rushabh Shah, Mackenzie Kelley, Kellan Wallace, Patricio Salazar, Devin Heath, Tori Linville, Jakob Salgado, Jeremiah Lee, Hannah Cushing, Thomas Craig, Kyla Pea, Katherine Bowers, Sara Vosoughi, Disha Patel, Matthew Gallo, Leah Gallo, Kristen Gallo, Jordan Andrews, Alyssa Sullivan, Cole McCarty, Jared Hughes, and William Linville. Thank you all.

About the Author

Abhi Kandukuru was born in North Florida, where he spent the majority of his childhood. At a young age he developed a strong passion for fantasy and a love of writing. Through influences from different movies, books and video/computer games, he created a character that faces adventure, magic and epic quests. From all of that and his own imagination comes our friend, Surya. As a 7th grade student at Walker middle magnet IB school, Abhi wrote on a variety of topics which gave him a broader view of the world. Eventually a story began to develop in his mind involving characters and places that he immediately grew attached to. Abhi knew that he needed to put his thoughts onto paper. He grew so intrigued with the evolving storyline that he knew he had to share his characters to the world. Abhi now lives in Central Florida with his family and is always supported by them in his writing career.